The Stillborn Lover

The Stillborn Lover
Timothy Findley

Blizzard Publishing • **Winnipeg**

The Stillborn Lover published by Blizzard Publishing Inc.
73 Furby Street, Winnipeg, MB Canada R3C 2A2
Originally hardcover edition published 1993, reprinted 1993.
This paperback edition published 1995.
© 1993 Pebble Productions Inc.

Printed in Canada by Freisen Printing Ltd.
Published with the assistance of
the Canada Council and the Manitoba Arts Council.

Caution

This play is fully protected under the copyright laws of Canada and all other
countries of the Copyright Union and is subject to royalty. Except in the
case of brief passages quoted in a review of this book, no part of this
publication (including cover design) may be reproduced or transmitted in any
form, by any means, electronic or mechanical, including recording, and
information storage and retrieval systems, without permission in writing
from the publisher, or, in the case of photocopying or other reprographic
copying, without a licence from Canadian Reprography Collective
(CANCOPY).

Rights to produce, in whole or part, by any group, amateur or profes-
sional, are retained by Pebble Productions Inc.

Canadian Cataloguing in Publication Data

Findley, Timothy, 1930–
  The stillborn lover
  ISBN 0-921368-33-X
I. Title.
PS8511.I38S74 1993   C812'.54   C93-098076-X
PR9199.3.F53S74 1993

For
Martha Henry
and
William Hutt

The Stillborn Lover was co-produced by The Grand Theatre, London, Ontario, and the National Arts Centre, Ottawa, Ontario, and premièred by The Grand Theatre on March 26, 1993, with the following cast:

HARRY	William Hutt
MARIAN	Martha Henry
MICHAEL	Donald Davis
JULIET	Patricia Collins
DIANA	Kate Trotter
JACKMAN	Hardee T. Lineham
MAHAVOLITCH	Michael McManus

Directed by Peter Moss
Set and costumes designed by Astrid Janson
Lighting designed by Paul Mathiesen
Original music by Boko Suzuki
Sound designed by Jim Neil
Stage Manager: Brian Scott
Assistant Stage Manager: Nancy Dryden

The Stillborn Lover opened at the National Arts Centre on April 29, 1993.

Characters

HARRY: Harry Raymond, Canadian Ambassador to Moscow; mid- to late-sixties.

MARIAN: Marian Raymond, his wife; late fifties.

DIANA: Diana Marsden, their daughter; a recently divorced lawyer, mid-twenties.

MICHAEL: Michael Riordon, Canada's Minister of External Affairs, touted as the next party leader; mid- to late-sixties.

JULIET: Juliet Riordon, his wife; late fifties, early sixties.

JACKMAN: Superintendent, RCMP B-Operations; forties.

MAHAVOLITCH: Corporal, RCMP, his junior partner; late twenties.

Set

Nominally, the setting is a safe house overlooking the Ottawa River at Rockcliffe. As the play unfolds, settings in other locations are evoked— a garden in Nagasaki, a courtyard and a bedroom in Cairo, a breakfast room and an antechamber in the Riordon house.

The set itself is a series of platforms, some of them angled, all of varying heights, and one of them, downstage, jutting out "dangerously" over the orchestra. Steps and walkways join the platforms.

Some wicker furniture, a garden bench, a bed, some louvered shutters, a great swatch of mosquito netting will be wanted. The rest is light and perhaps, projected silhouettes—a palm tree, a window, a tiled roof, etc.

Music is provided by guitar, piano and flute.

The action of the play takes place in 1972 and earlier, to the 1940s.

Prelude

(The house is perched on a steep ravine that drops down to a river. The house appears to float in space—insubstantial, tenuous— adrift amongst autumn trees that fade toward distant hills.

Music: Flute—with a Japanese flavour accompanies and supports the following, which may, as in the original production, be a spoken voice-over.)

MARIAN: In Japan, there is an ancient game called Go. Its ritual moves are played on a squared-off board. Every move is made with a round, smooth stone. Once the stones have been set in place, they cannot be withdrawn. Their positions are locked, irrevocable. Like the moves and gestures we make with our lives.

(The lights fade. The music concludes on a single, drifting note.)

Act One

Scene One

(Autumn. Late afternoon. On one of the platforms, wicker furniture is piled beneath dust cloths. Downstage, there is a stone bench. The stage is empty of people. Far off, a dog barks. Silence.)

JULIET: *(Off.)* How lovely! I'd forgotten.

DIANA: *(Off.)* I can't believe you'd give it up ...

JULIET: *(Off.)* I can't believe it either.

DIANA: *(Off.)* Do we have to go in through the house? Can't we go this way?

MICHAEL: *(Off.)* I don't see why not.

>*(DIANA enters the garden. She wears a tailored overcoat and a dark beret with a diamond pin on it.)*

DIANA: Oh ... Wonderful.

>*(MICHAEL enters—pausing to let the others pass before him.)*

MICHAEL: You care for that, Diana?

DIANA: Yes. Oh, yes. Father? Do come ... The view!

>*(JULIET enters—followed by HARRY. All are wearing lightweight overcoats—autumn clothing.)*

JULIET: There you go, Harry. Diana wants to show you the river.

>*(HARRY crosses to DIANA. JULIET lets him pass, hanging back near MICHAEL.)*

DIANA: Don't look till you get here, father. Don't. There. How about that!

HARRY: Yes ...

DIANA: Nothing anywhere beats the view up that river. Not in October.

JULIET: *(Taking MICHAEL's arm.)* We were so happy here. Weren't we, Mike—all those years ago. Of all the houses everywhere in our lives, we were never better off than here.

MICHAEL: True enough. I guess ...

> *(MAHAVOLITCH and JACKMAN enter. Both wear rain coats and both carry hand luggage—MAHAVOLITCH a good deal more than JACKMAN.)*

I'm afraid you'll have to take that in the other way.

MAHAVOLITCH: Yessir.

> *(MAHAVOLITCH and JACKMAN prepare to exit.)*

MICHAEL: Once you're inside, you might unlock that door. *(Referring to the sunroom, where furniture is piled.)* Where's Mrs. Raymond?

JACKMAN: Can't say, Minister. Thought she'd come around with you and Ambassador Raymond.

MICHAEL: No. No. *(He looks at RAYMOND.)* Harry?

HARRY: Yes, Mike ... *(Slight pause.)* What is it?

JULIET: Where's Marian?

HARRY: I don't know. Didn't she ...?

DIANA: *(Breaks away, calling.)* Mother ...?

MICHAEL: She can't have gone far ...

> *(MAHAVOLITCH and JACKMAN start to set down the luggage.)*

No. Get them into the house. We'll find Mrs. Raymond.

MAHAVOLITCH: Yes, Minister.

> *(They exit—with luggage—JACKMAN again making sure that MAHAVOLITCH carries most of it.*
>
> *MICHAEL watches HARRY, who has not moved from his place.)*

HARRY: *(Finally.)* I don't understand. Marian was definitely with us.

DIANA: *(Calling.)* Mother ...?

> *(She exits.)*

HARRY: ... I'm sure of it.

JULIET: Not to worry.

HARRY: Marian?

JULIET: No. Let me ... Diana and I will find her.

(She starts to exit.)

HARRY: Thank you, Juliet. *(Pause.)* I'm sorry, Mike.

MICHAEL: She'll turn up. *(He looks around the garden.)* You know, it's quite true. I guess we were happier here in this house than anywhere else we've ever lived ... me and Juliet. And we've certainly had our share of cities. Santiago, Moscow, London ...

> *(MAHAVOLITCH and JACKMAN appear in the sunroom and unlock the doors—after which they begin to arrange the furniture, taking off the dust sheets, etc. MICHAEL looks at the river.)*

Imagine, after all that—to say you were happiest in Ottawa, of all places. But, oh dear God ... those hills—that river ... and, of course, our children were born here.

HARRY: Yes.

MICHAEL: Diana was born ... Where was it? Japan?

HARRY: That's right.

MICHAEL: Nagasaki?

HARRY: Yes.

MICHAEL: Wonderful, isn't it—the useless information a person stores.

HARRY: Next thing you know, you'll remember where you were born.

MICHAEL: I'm sorry. That was completely thoughtless.

HARRY: Yes, it was, But I forgive you ... *(He smiles.)*

MICHAEL: *(Smiling.)* Thank you.

DIANA/JULIET: *(Off.)* Mother ...? Marian ...?

MICHAEL: *(Pause.)* Have you talked with her ... with Marian ... about why you might be here?

HARRY: How could I do that? I don't know why we're here. *(Pause.)* All we were told was: I've been called home on "special duty."

MICHAEL: Yes. Well.

HARRY: I guess we all know what that means.

MICHAEL: *(Making light of it.)* Do we, now.

HARRY: Oh, for Christ's sake, Mike. Being called home on "special duty" is just a polite way of saying there's going to be an investigation. What I don't know is why.

> *(Offstage, the dog barks again in the distance.)*

Why are we here, Mike? And at whose instigation?

(MICHAEL does not answer.)

Was it yours?

MICHAEL: I'm only a servant, Harry. Just a servant—like you.

HARRY: Like hell you are. You're bloody Minister of External Affairs.

MICHAEL: Yes. But in matters like these, the bloody Minister of External Affairs is still just a servant. We will talk about it tomorrow.

HARRY: But …

MICHAEL: *Tomorrow. (Beat.)* Today, rest. That's a hell of a journey you've just made. Moscow to here—non-stop.

JULIET/DIANA: *(Off.)* Marian …? Mother …?

HARRY: Yes. I'm tired.

JULIET: *(Off.)* Yoo-hoo! Marian …?

MICHAEL: What about this, Harry? Disappearing like this …

HARRY: Marian? It's part of her condition.

MICHAEL: Ah …

HARRY: Yes. Alzheimer's. The disease with no design. Plays havoc with the memory. Like this—being lost. In Moscow, she would disappear for hours. It was nerve-wracking. Once, she came back to the Embassy with blood on her dress. "Where have you been?" "I don't know." "Why is there blood?" "I don't know." The good thing is—so far—she's always managed to find her way home.

MICHAEL: Thank god for that.

HARRY: *(Lightly.)* We're coping, of course. Oh, yes—sometimes we don't even know when she's in the disease. I don't know—she doesn't. And there's no medication. But we're coping. We're coping.

MICHAEL: I'm sorry, Harry. I am. Look, you must have an A-1 case of jet lag. Let's just … celebrate the fact you're here. Shall we? *(Indicates the sunroom.)* Why don't you and I find a drink?

(They go to the steps, HARRY hanging back.)

She'll turn up. They'll find her.

(MICHAEL and HARRY join MAHAVOLITCH and JACKMAN in the sunroom. MICHAEL says a few words to them and then leads HARRY up the stairway into the body of the house.)

Scene Two

(Music: A chord that lingers.)

DIANA/JULIET: *(Off.)* Mother ...? Marian ...?

(Music: A second chord.)

Marian ...? Mother ...?

(MARIAN enters. She carries an open umbrella and a bouquet of flowers wrapped in paper. She looks at the garden around her and then she stares at the river.

Music: A resolving chord.

MARIAN closes her eyes and wavers.

DIANA enters.)

DIANA: Mother ...

MARIAN: Where have you been, Diana? I've been looking for you everywhere.

DIANA: *(Laughs.)* I've been looking for you!

MARIAN: Aren't you cold? I thought I heard Juliet.

DIANA: You did. She's ... Mother, you can put the umbrella down. It's not raining. *(DIANA does this for her.)* And do you want me to hold the flowers? *(Takes them.)*

MARIAN: Just remember they're mine.

(She sits on the garden bench, placing umbrella beneath it.)

All the leaves are turning red. Winter's coming. Not my favourite. Maybe the reason they've brought us back is to give your father a posting in the sun. You think? Perhaps ...?

DIANA: I can't answer that. Everything happened so quickly. I got a phone call: "Your parents are arriving. Come to Uplands!" That's really all I know.

MARIAN: *(Merely saying it.)* Liar ...

DIANA: It's true, mother. I can't tell you anything ...

(Still at some distance, the dog barks.

MARIAN waves her hand for silence. DIANA listens.)

It's only some dog. Down by the river. *(Beat.)* All I know is, you're here—and I'm glad you're here.

MARIAN: Is he lost, that dog? Look—there's Juliet.

(JULIET enters.)

Somebody's lost their dog. Is it yours? Were you looking? Is that where you've been all this time? Have you seen the house? Whose is it? Maybe it's their dog. Whoever lives here ...

DIANA: I don't really think so, mother. The house has been empty a long time. This is where you're going to be staying—you and father—until we know what's going to happen next.

MARIAN: I hope what happens next is somewhere in the sun. Anywhere but ... *what's-its-face* ...

DIANA: Australia, maybe. You haven't had Australia.

MARIAN: *(Ignoring DIANA.)* Did you ever have to suffer the wonders of *what's-its-face,* Juliet?

JULIET: *What's-it ... where?*

(She looks at DIANA.)

DIANA: Moscow.

MARIAN: What makes you so certain I mean Moscow? *(Turning.)* Have you, Juliet?

JULIET: What?

MARIAN: Been there?

JULIET: Where?

MARIAN: *Moscow.*

JULIET: Yes. That was our last posting ...

MARIAN: Muscovites are pigs ...

JULIET: ... before Mike became Minister.

MARIAN: Swine.

JULIET: Yes—well ... We rather enjoyed it there. I think it's one of the most beautiful embassies we have.

MARIAN: We haven't been to India. Maybe they'll give us India. You think?

DIANA: Maybe there won't be a posting at all. Maybe they'll let you rest for a while.

MARIAN: Rest? Not here, pray God.

DIANA: I think father looks tired. Don't you, Juliet?

MARIAN: We will not rest here. *(Listens.)* Oh, that poor dog ...

JULIET: Whether you end up in India or Timbuktu isn't something for us to decide. That's what I've always loved most about External ... someone else makes all your decisions. The only thing you have to do is catch the right plane. *(To DIANA.)* Let me take those ... *(Takes flowers; speaks quietly.)* Don't you think we should get her inside?

(MARIAN suddenly walks downstage.

MICHAEL comes into the sunroom carrying a drink and an 8 x 10 government issue envelope with seals. He has removed his topcoat. MAHAVOLITCH and JACKMAN have finished setting the furniture in place. Whatever conversation they have with MICHAEL is not heard—but their talk is obviously about the Raymonds— HARRY, somewhere in the house, and MARIAN, in the garden. Also about the contents of the envelope, which MICHAEL passes to JACKMAN.)

MARIAN: I heard that. I don't want to go inside. You know—I swear I've been in this garden before.

JULIET: You have.

MARIAN: That view. The river ...

(She moves onto the jutting platform.)

JULIET: Mike and I lived here after the war. You came to visit us when Diana was still a baby. You'd just returned from Japan.

MARIAN: There was a swing over there ...

JULIET: That's right ...

MARIAN: Hanging from that tree ...

JULIET: That's right ...

DIANA: What tree?

MARIAN: And I used to swing ... way out over the edge.

DIANA: What tree? Where?

JULIET: We cut it down.

MARIAN: And the view was ...

DIANA: Isn't that funny ...

MARIAN: *(At the edge.)* ... electrifying ...

(HARRY, minus topcoat, appears on one of the upper platforms. He looks down into the garden.)

DIANA: I don't remember any tree ...

MARIAN: Wonderful! You could swing right into the sky.

DIANA: ... why did you cut it down?

JULIET: It was old, I guess. I don't remember.

MARIAN: Dangerous and marvelous! I used to have dreams about letting go. Just letting go and sailing out over that ravine ... *kerplop!*

> *(DIANA laughs.)*

With you in my lap.

DIANA: Me?

MARIAN: Yes. Baby Diana—in her swaddling clothes.

DIANA: But only in your dreams ...

MARIAN: Don't be afraid. I never let go of you. Not for an instant.

DIANA: Well—thank you. Did we ... *land?*

MARIAN: But, of course.

DIANA: In my dreams—when I'm falling, I never land.

MARIAN: Well—in my dreams, I do.

JULIET: *Kerplop ...*

> *(DIANA shoots JULIET a look. JULIET shrugs and smiles. HARRY moves away from window.)*

DIANA: *(To MARIAN.)* Are we destroyed?

MARIAN: Destroyed?

DIANA: When we land ... are we killed?

MARIAN: Well, of course we are. You don't think you could fall that distance and not be killed, do you?

DIANA: No. But in dreams, things are different ...

MARIAN: Tell her, Juliet ... how we used to sail out over that ravine. She doesn't believe me.

JULIET: All I remember is the tree ...

MARIAN: *(Dispassionate.)* Liar.

> *(HARRY exits.)*

JULIET: And the swing, of course. I remember the swing.

> *(MICHAEL comes to the edge of the sunroom.)*

MICHAEL: How would you ladies like to come in and have a drink ... take a look around?

> *(MAHAVOLITCH and JACKMAN exit.)*

JULIET: Good idea. It's getting cold. *(Turns.)* I'm going to put these in water.

> *(JULIET makes for the steps, but MARIAN and DIANA hang back.)*

Is the inside still as lovely as it was?

MICHAEL: A little barren perhaps. But we can rectify all that.

> *(JULIET exits.*
>
> *The dog barks in the ravine.)*

MARIAN: Maybe he's found our shattered bones, Diana—yours and mine—hidden all these years beneath the leaves.

> *(MARIAN turns and heads for the sunroom.*
>
> *DIANA remains downstage.*
>
> *HARRY enters the sunroom carrying a tray with bottles and glasses on it.)*

HARRY: One thing about a safe house, Mike—wherever they are, whatever their purpose—they always have best liquor.

MICHAEL: Yes. And plenty of it.

> *(MARIAN has been on the instant of entering the sunroom, but she stops in her tracks.)*

MARIAN: Safe house? Did Harry say *safe house?*

> *(No one answers.*
>
> *Hold.*
>
> *The lights fade—except on DIANA, downstage.)*

Scene Three

> *(DIANA crosses to the jutting edge and stares down into the ravine.*
>
> *JACKMAN comes into the garden from the side of the house. He watches her for a moment.)*

JACKMAN: Steep, isn't it.

DIANA: Yes.

JACKMAN: Sometimes—not very often—you get the smell of sulfur from the other side of the river. The pulp mills.

DIANA: Yes.

JACKMAN: Otherwise, beautiful. The perfect location.

DIANA: What for?

JACKMAN: Sorry?

DIANA: Perfect location for what?

JACKMAN: Well—the view, of course.

DIANA: Of the river—or my parents? You're with the RCMP, aren't you.

JACKMAN: You've got it, Miss Raymond.

DIANA: *(Into garden.)* I'm not Miss Raymond.

JACKMAN: Well ...

DIANA: My name is Marsden. Diana Marsden. And what's your name?

JACKMAN: Jackman.

DIANA: Is that it? Just Jackman?

JACKMAN: Superintendent Jackman, RCMP.

DIANA: Yes—I was forgetting. You people never do have first names, do you.

JACKMAN: Danny ...

DIANA: It doesn't really suit you does it: *Danny* ...

JACKMAN: Well—it's *Daniel,* to be right about it. But I've had *Danny* all my life. What name might you find more suitable, Mrs. Marsden?

DIANA: Oh—I don't now. Clint, or something. Burt.

JACKMAN: I see. So your impression of me is just about the same as my impression of you: *wrong.*

DIANA: What do you mean by that?

JACKMAN: That I *did* know your name was Marsden ... if it matters. But you've been divorced and I thought you must've reverted. Most women do, these days. Revert to their maiden name.

DIANA: I'm not, and never was a maiden, Superintendent.

JACKMAN: Well. Score one for you.

DIANA: So ... what else *don't* you know about me?

JACKMAN: Not much, I guess. Maybe what colour your underwear is. I *do* know how many husbands you've had and why you divorced them. What books you read. What pills you take—and why. The fact that you're a lawyer. I could name all your clients, if you want me to ...

DIANA: No thank you.

JACKMAN: I know how many cases you've won—how many you've lost—how much money you make. What sort of clients you prefer ...

DIANA: You're very thorough.

JACKMAN: It's my job, Mrs. Marsden. There's more, if you want to hear it.

DIANA: No.

JACKMAN: I wouldn't want you to think your father and mother were in careless hands.

DIANA: Are they in protective custody? Surely you can tell me that. Are they in danger?

JACKMAN: There's all kinds of danger, Mrs. Marsden. Isn't there. *(He smiles.)*

> *(DIANA stares at him for a moment—and then she crosses to the steps. In the sunroom, muted voices are raised.)*

DIANA: Are you coming in, Superintendent?

JACKMAN: Not just yet.

DIANA: I wish I could say it had been a pleasure talking to you.

JACKMAN: No you don't, ma'am. But I'll accept the sentiment.

> *(DIANA goes up the steps and into the sunroom. There is another burst of voices. MARIAN hurries to her and takes her arm as if Diana's presence will make everything all right. JACKMAN goes to the edge and looks into the ravine.*
>
> *Pause. The dog barks.*
>
> *JACKMAN brightens. He nods—as if in response to a signal from below. Then he waves.*
>
> *The lights dim.)*

Scene Four

> *(Sunroom.*
>
> *MARIAN removes her outer coat and puts it first over one chair and then another. She then becomes preoccupied with a spot on her collar—her back to the audience.)*

HARRY: Good for you, Diana. I was beginning to think you'd deserted us. Have a drink.

DIANA: Thank you, father. Is mother ...?

(HARRY pours DIANA a drink.)

HARRY: *(Ignores her question.)* We were just discussing futures.

DIANA: Futures—yes. Exciting—for some. *(To MICHAEL.)* You're to be the next PM, I understand.

MICHAEL: Nothing is certain.

DIANA: How could they resist you, Michael. I think it's splendid. Your health.

MICHAEL: Thank you, Diana.

HARRY: When does it happen?

MICHAEL: The convention is in four weeks. Slightly less.

HARRY: And you're a shoo-in?

MICHAEL: So they tell me.

HARRY: I'm out of touch.

MICHAEL: Not really. The momentum is fairly recent. Two months ago, we thought he was going to get better.

HARRY: The Prime Minister.

MICHAEL: Yes. It *is* a cancer. Inoperable. Nothing's being said. Just that he wants to spend more time with his family. The usual—write his memoirs—enjoy the sunset.

HARRY: He's been Prime Minister eight years.

MICHAEL: Yes. And it's been a good eight years. Good for him—good for the country—and very good for the Party.

(JULIET enters with the flowers in a vase.)

HARRY: How old is he now?

JULIET: Who?

MICHAEL: The PM.

MARIAN: *(Not turning.)* Seventy-one.

(Everyone looks at her. She is unaware of it, concentrating on the spot.)

JULIET: *(Showing flowers.)* Aren't they beautiful.

MARIAN: Where did you get those?

JULIET: Why, I …

MARIAN: They're mine.

JULIET: Of course they are, dear. I gave them to you when you got off the plane. Remember? I was just putting them in water.

(She sets flowers on a table.)

MARIAN: Everyone keeps taking everything. Where's my umbrella?

DIANA: I thought you had it, mother.

MARIAN: You had it.

DIANA: No. I folded it up and gave it back to you, in the garden.

MARIAN: When?

JULIET: I wouldn't worry about your umbrella, dear. It hasn't rained here in days.

MARIAN: Do you call everyone "dear," Juliet? Or just people you don't like?

JULIET: *(Getting a drink.)* My goodness. We are cranky, aren't we ...

MARIAN: I heard that. First I'm "dear"—and then I'm "we." People have names, Juliet.

JULIET: Yes, Marian.

MARIAN: I also happen not to be crazy.

JULIET: No one said you were.

MARIAN: You said cranky. Cranky means crazy.

DIANA: *(Laughing.)* Oh—mother—for heaven's sake!

MARIAN: It's German, *Krankenhaus.* That's the crazy-house. The loony bin.

(HARRY walks away. He cannot bear this. MICHAEL watches him.)

JULIET: *(To MICHAEL.)* Should we leave? *(Smiles.)* Let these people get some rest ...?

HARRY: No. Please. Finish your drinks.

(MAHAVOLITCH and JACKMAN enter the garden. JACKMAN sits on the bench, facing front. MAHAVOLITCH swings an imaginary golf club.)

MAHAVOLITCH: Whammo!

JACKMAN: You missed.

(MAHAVOLITCH sits on the bench facing the sunroom.)

JULIET: Well! The election process begins. Tomorrow night, cocktails and a dinner party. Sixty people. Under our own roof! Can you believe it? I thought we'd done all that in our embassy days. But ... *(Waves her hands.)* here we go again. Of course, it's different when you have a staff—the way you do when you're abroad. Still—I've got help coming in. Call themselves The Commissariats. Sounds like a Russian rock band, to me. They're kids. Students. They never know where anything is. They offer to bring their own stuff but I said yes to that, once, and the silly twits turned up with paper plates. Plastic utensils. And plastic champagne glasses. I said: "We aren't serving champagne." One of the girls made a face and said: "I thought this was going to be a class act." It's because we're in North America, of course. You wouldn't catch a Brit with a paper plate! Not in ten million ... Well. I did once. But it was the American Embassy. A garden party. There's some excuse for that. If you're celebrating Walt Disney's birthday—and all the guests are two.

DIANA: My goodness, Juliet. Sixty. Where will you seat them all?

JULIET: Garden tables.

DIANA: In this weather?

JULIET: No, no, Diana. Indoors. But at garden tables. I saw it in a magazine. I thought it was so clever. Garden furniture is so sturdy. Nice big round tables—lovely little chairs. Everything white ...

MICHAEL: Classy. *(He winks at HARRY.)*

JULIET: Yes. Well. Ingenuity. That's what counts. I dread it, of course. The dear PM with his dire disease will be there. He's being wonderful to Mike—absolutely wonderful. Shows up—even in pain—and waves the flag. This thing tomorrow is a mix of the converted and the unconverted. What Michael calls the Party-*pros* and the Party-*poopers.*

MARIAN: The *patsies* and the *shit-disturbers.*

JULIET: That's right, Marian. Call a spade a spade. *(Beat.)* Of course, it's different, now that we're in politics. The rules are different. As the ambassador's wife, I used to memorize people's faces. Now, as the candidate's wife, I memorize their shoes. In politics, every time you turn around, there's a whole new set of toes not to step on. Yes, Michael?

> *(MICHAEL waves his hand.)*

And the obfuscation! The manipulation! The first thing I learned when we got back to Ottawa was that I didn't have to smile any more when I told a lie. Abroad, as the Ambassador's wife, I used to think of cocktail parties as *discretion-sessions.* Here, we have *deception-*

receptions. Shocking. But then, I'm the one who used to think that gerrymandering meant *taking care of the Germans* ...

MICHAEL: It does—in Germany.

JULIET: I think we'd better leave.

MICHAEL: Yes.

MARIAN: This event, Juliet—what is it, tomorrow?

JULIET: A dinner party.

MARIAN: Are we invited?

(No one knows what to say.)

DIANA: You're having dinner with me, tomorrow, mother. Good-bye, Juliet. Michael.

JULIET: Good-bye, all.

MICHAEL: *(Aside.)* Walk me to the front door, Harry. You're right. We need to have a word.

HARRY: Certainly.

MICHAEL: You go on ahead, Juliet. I'll be with you in a moment.

(The lights fade slightly in the sunroom as HARRY leads MICHAEL and JULIET off. MARIAN stands and stares out the window. DIANA watches her.)

MAHAVOLITCH: *(Turning front.)* So. When do we begin?

JACKMAN: We already have.

MAHAVOLITCH: Oh? How?

JACKMAN: Just go on sitting here. It makes them nervous.

(JULIET appears on one of the walkways between platforms. She is putting on her gloves in obvious distress.)

JULIET: Shit. *(She looks back.)*

(MICHAEL enters behind her.)

You didn't have to make me do that.

MICHAEL: Do what?

JULIET: Prattle.

MICHAEL: It's your great, good talent, Juliet. Be grateful.

JULIET: But they're our friends.

MICHAEL: Precisely.

JULIET: You don't prattle at friends, Mike.

MICHAEL: You do when they're in trouble.

JULIET: Oh, god. That poor woman. *(She takes his arm.)* I've never seen a woman so obviously distressed. She nearly bit my head off.

MICHAEL: Yes.

JULIET: She doesn't know yet, does she. Why they're here.

MICHAEL: No. I've only just told Harry. Now—he will tell her. And Diana.

JULIET: What? What will he tell them?

MICHAEL: *(Stops, looks at her.)* Harry and Marian are here, Juliet. They've come home. That's all I can tell you.

> *(MICHAEL exits. JULIET looks back at the sunroom and at MARIAN. Then she exits.)*

MARIAN: There are two men out there.

DIANA: Yes.

MARIAN: I want to go home.

DIANA: We are home, mother.

> *(The lights fade altogether on the two women.)*

MAHAVOLITCH: Somebody left their umbrella behind.

> *(He has found the umbrella under the bench. Now, he raises it. They sit for a moment. Then JACKMAN puts his hand out, palm up.)*

JACKMAN: You're right. It's raining.

> *(MAHAVOLITCH does the same.)*

MAHAVOLITCH: No, it's not.

JACKMAN: Yes, it is.

MAHAVOLITCH: No, it's not.

> *(JACKMAN rises.)*

JACKMAN: Yes. It is, Corporal Mahavolitch.

> *(Takes umbrella and holds it over himself.)*

It is pouring.

> *(MAHAVOLITCH slowly rises.)*

Come on.

(As they exit, MAHAVOLITCH looks at the sky, shrugs, and turns his collar up.

Music: Segue.)

Scene Five

(Sunroom. MARIAN stands where she was, staring at the garden. DIANA is near the vase of flowers.

HARRY enters. Michael has now told him why he has been brought home. He is agitated, hyperactive. He crosses to table where bottles and glasses and ice await him. He prepares a drink for each of them.)

DIANA: *(To HARRY.)* So. Now what?

HARRY: Now, we wait.

DIANA: What for?

HARRY: To hear what they have to say. In the morning.

DIANA: You don't know what they're going to say?

HARRY: *(Lying.)* No. Not precisely.

DIANA: What about mother?

HARRY: Your mother will be fine. She needs to rest.

DIANA: *(Accepting drink.)* Look at her. So still. I had no idea she was so badly off. It must be very hard on you, father.

HARRY: Yes. But worse, of course, for her.

> *(HARRY approaches MARIAN with her drink. She does not move or look at him.)*

Marian?

MARIAN: Why have they brought us here, Harry?

HARRY: I don't know, yet. They haven't told me.

MARIAN: Liar.

> *(She looks at him. He offers her the drink. She ignores it.)*

You think I don't know what a safe house is for?

> *(She takes cigarettes from her handbag—gets one out and looks for her lighter.)*

I do remember *some* things, you know. It's not *all* gone, up here. I do remember *some* things ...

> *(She cannot find her lighter.)*

HARRY: Of course you do.

MARIAN: Don't you patronize me, you bastard. Why are they hiding us? Why are we being hidden, Harry? They found you out, didn't they. How? What have you done?

> *(DIANA is watching HARRY.)*

HARRY: Nothing.

MARIAN: We're not in hiding for "nothing," Harry.

HARRY: Don't stare at me, Diana. Light your mother's cigarette.

> *(HARRY puts Marian's drink on a nearby table and goes back to the drinks table. DIANA lights Marian's cigarette. MARIAN looks at DIANA through her smoke.)*

MARIAN: Do you call that thing a hat?

DIANA: I call it a beret.

MARIAN: Does that pin thing belong to me?

DIANA: No, mother. It's mine.

MARIAN: *(Picking up drink.)* I never wear hats. I hate them. The only reason people wear hats is because they have something to hide. Are you going bald?

DIANA: No, mother.

> *(MARIAN leans in close to DIANA and whispers.)*

MARIAN: Do you know why we're here?

DIANA: No.

MARIAN: It's a posting. They're going to give us another posting.

> *(HARRY coughs.)*

Why can't we go to Mexico? I want to go to Mexico. Hot white sand. Cool white houses. In Cairo ... In Cairo we had red tile floors and ceiling fans. Balconies. I sat in the sun for days on end. Your father loved it there ... Didn't you, Harry—love it there in Cairo.

HARRY: Yes.

MARIAN: Diana says they're giving us Mexico.

> *(HARRY glances at DIANA. DIANA shakes her head.)*

Won't that be wonderful? Just to get out of the cold. That's all I want.

HARRY: We've done Mexico, Marian. Years ago.

MARIAN: Have we?

HARRY: Yes. *(Beat.)* They'll tell you this in the morning, anyhow. I might as well tell you now.

MARIAN: What? Another lie?

HARRY: No. Not a lie. *(Beat.)* Mike just told me. *(Beat.)*

> *(MAHAVOLITCH appears on an upper level. Puts a suitcase on floor. He begins to undress. There is a straight-back chair for him to lay clothing on.)*

There's been a killing. In Moscow. A young man. They found the body in a hotel room.

DIANA: So?

HARRY: Questions are being asked.

DIANA: *(Comes down stairs.)* Why? Was he a Canadian? One of your staff?

HARRY: No.

DIANA: Then—what's it got to do with you? *(Beat.)* Did you know him? Did mother know him? What's the connection?

HARRY: He was murdered ...

> *(MAHAVOLITCH by now is shirtless.)*

DIANA: But what's that got to do with you and mother being returned to Canada?

MARIAN: It was him, wasn't it, Harry. *(Sits.)*

> *(MAHAVOLITCH undoes his belt and zipper.)*

HARRY: Yes.

DIANA: Who?

MARIAN: Mischa ...

> *(MAHAVOLITCH kicks off his loafers.)*

DIANA: Daddy?

> *(MAHAVOLITCH "freezes."*
>
> *The stair-door opens. JACKMAN enters the sunroom.)*

JACKMAN: Excuse me?

HARRY: I said we wanted to be alone!

JACKMAN: Sorry. We found this umbrella.

> *(He leaves it and exits.)*

MARIAN: Bang.

HARRY: What?

MARIAN: *Bang!* The umbrella just exploded.

DIANA: Tell me who he was. The young man—the dead man.

   (MAHAVOLITCH removes his trousers.)

 Who *was* he? Mother knew his name.

   (HARRY walks away.)

MARIAN: He was a friend. Of mine. *(Beat.)* Of your father's.

DIANA: Murdered?

HARRY: Yes.

DIANA: My god.

HARRY: Indeed.

   (DIANA looks at MARIAN. Suddenly, DIANA sits down. She closes her eyes. When she opens them, she stares at HARRY with her hand across her mouth.)

HARRY: We know nothing, Diana. Nothing.

MARIAN: *(Quietly.)* Liar.

   (The lights fade in the sunroom.)

Scene Six

(MAHAVOLITCH, now in his shorts, crouches by his suitcase. He opens it and removes his service revolver. Then he stands up and straps it on with a shoulder holster. He crosses to an imaginary mirror, his back to the audience. Watching himself, he removes his shorts and stands there—contented.

Music: A conclusion.

Lights fade on upper platform.)

Scene Seven

(Walkway. Evening. DIANA alone. Her beret is off, her coat around her shoulders.

In the sunroom, MARIAN rises.)

MARIAN: Why didn't you tell me? *(Begins to exit.)* Why didn't you tell me?

HARRY: *(Following her.)* How could I tell you? I didn't know.

(Both exit.)

MARIAN: *(Off.)* Oh, god. Dead.

> *(There is the sound of a door closing.*
>
> *DIANA sighs.*
>
> *JACKMAN enters—on a different level or platform.)*

JACKMAN: A bit cool to be standing about.

DIANA: I don't mind. Where's your friend?

JACKMAN: Gone running. He's a health nut.

DIANA: Ah—yes.

JACKMAN: Not my style. Never was. Give me an armchair every time. May I join you?

DIANA: You already have.

JACKMAN: *(With humour.)* Is it me you don't like? Or just men?

DIANA: You.

> *(JACKMAN moves to her vicinity.)*

And you? Is it me you like? Or just women?

JACKMAN: Women.

DIANA: Thank heaven for that.

JACKMAN: Pleasant evening—in spite of the cool.

DIANA: I was counting stars.

JACKMAN: *(Looking.)* There only is one.

DIANA: That's right. One.

JACKMAN: When you get to *two,* let me know.

DIANA: Two now—if the moon is a star.

JACKMAN: No. The moon is just the moon, ma'am. *(Pause.)* It was decent of you to stay on. They'll be needing you.

DIANA: I was told to stay on.

JACKMAN: Oh—really?

DIANA: Yes. By the Minister—and you know it. Don't play pussy-foot with me, Superintendent. Why don't you ask your first question?

JACKMAN: You know why they're here? Why they've been brought back?

DIANA: There's a dead man.

JACKMAN: That's right. A young Russian.

DIANA: I gather my parents knew him.

JACKMAN: Yes. They did.

DIANA: This young man, so I gather, was murdered. He was a friend of my mother's. Has my father been accused of this?

JACKMAN: Not yet.

DIANA: But he's a suspect.

JACKMAN: You've got it.

DIANA: But that's preposterous. What makes you think my father could commit a murder?

JACKMAN: What makes you think he couldn't?

DIANA: Oh, *please.*

(She moves away from him.)

JACKMAN: *(Amused.)* That doesn't sound much like a lawyer's answer, Mrs. Marsden. Sounds more like a daughter's answer to me.

DIANA: I am a daughter. First and foremost—where my parents are concerned.

JACKMAN: Yes, ma'am.

DIANA: Must you call me "ma'am"?

JACKMAN: Yes, ma'am.

DIANA: You sound like a boy scout.

JACKMAN: There you are then. Me "boy scout." You "daughter." *(Beat.)* Any chance the policeman might get an answer from the lawyer?

DIANA: Not a chance in hell.

JACKMAN: You mean you aren't prepared to weigh the evidence?

DIANA: What evidence?

JACKMAN: Your father was *there,* Mrs. Marsden. Your father was there. The boy was not a stranger to him. What if ...?

DIANA: What if *what?*

JACKMAN: What if he killed him in self-defense? People do that, you know. Even good people.

DIANA: *(Cool.)* Go on. Educate me.

JACKMAN: Put it this way, Mrs. Marsden: right now, you yourself are engaged in self-defense. It all depends how far the self extends, doesn't it ...

(MARIAN enters the garden—moonlit.)

Some people think of their parents as being a part of themselves. Yes?
Parents think of their children that way. Husbands. Wives. Extensions
of the self. So, when it comes to self-defense ... You see my point, I
trust.

(DIANA has been watching MARIAN.)

DIANA: *(Quietly.)* Yes. I see your point. *(Pause.)* My mother ... My
father ... My parents, Mister Jackman, are *(Smiles.) uncommon folk.*
Exceptional. They actually love one another. Can you imagine that?
I regard them with a sense, I guess, of wonder—given what they've
survived.

JACKMAN: You're telling me you love them.

DIANA: No. Respect—yes. Love? I'm not so sure.

JACKMAN: They been married long?

DIANA: Since the war. You know all this. You must've read the brief.

JACKMAN: It says you were born in Japan. Nagasaki.

DIANA: That's right. Nagasaki is where they went on their honeymoon,
if you can believe it. That's what they were like. Idealists. Later, they
went back, just so I could be born there. I think I was their gesture of
atonement.

MARIAN: Harry?

JACKMAN: Your dad was in Japan with some sort of commission.

DIANA: Yes. *(Playing it.)* The Canadian Mission to the Supreme Com-
mander for the Allied Powers for the Occupation and Control of
Japan! SCAP!

MARIAN: Harry? Come out and see the moon.

DIANA: Mother was with them, too. As a cipher clerk.

(HARRY enters garden.)

They were in their thirties, then. Young ...

(Music: Flute—a Japanese melody.

*HARRY stands behind MARIAN with his hand on her shoulder.
They look at the moon.)*

Do you ever try to imagine your parents, Superintendent ... what they
were like before you were born?

(Lights alter.)

MARIAN: *(Younger.)* Tell me why you came to Japan.

HARRY: *(Younger.)* I was posted here. I had no choice.

MARIAN: Oh, come on. You could've said no.

HARRY: I didn't want to say *no*. I wanted to be here. I wanted to see what had been done. I didn't want to be "told," any more. We were being told so many lies.

MARIAN: You knew they were lies?

HARRY: Yes. Discretionary lies, of course.

MARIAN: About the bombs?

HARRY: Yes. *(Beat.)* You said *bombs*. Plural. That's interesting.

MARIAN: You think so?

HARRY: Yes.

MARIAN: It was deliberate. I say it to test the waters—see who I'm talking to. Most people let it pass. They don't even notice. What is it, now—not quite a year since they fell?

HARRY: Ten months, six days ...

MARIAN: And ten months, three days. One—and then the other. Hiroshima. Nagasaki. The Japanese had already sued for peace before the first bomb fell. Did you know that?

HARRY: Perhaps you shouldn't be telling me this. Aren't things like that official secrets?

MARIAN: The war is over, Harry. I can tell you anything I like. About the war. Not about now, of course. Funny, isn't it. Here we are married—the cipher clerk and the junior diplomat—sworn to silence. What will we talk about in bed at night? Not our secrets. *Never.* Never our secrets. Only our lies. *(Laughs.)* Unless, of course, we talk in our sleep.

HARRY: The burden must have been unbearable, during the war. For you.

MARIAN: Yes. And no. It was just a job—if you didn't think about it. When you did think about it—what you knew—it was dreadful. Knowing when people would die. Hundreds of them—without warning ... There were moments ... There were moments when I wanted ... wanted to stand in the street and shout out the truth. Which, of course, one never did. Sometimes, what you knew was wonderful. Like the suit for peace. It was July—last year: July, 1945—still not a year ago—good Lord! I was in England, then—a cipher clerk at Bletchley Park—part of a special liaison unit decoding intercepts sent on to us by the Americans. This particular intercept was of a message sent from Tokyo to the Japanese Embassy in Moscow. The Emperor had "brought his will to bear in favour of peace." Isn't that wonderful? The language of desperate diplomacy: *brought his will to bear in favour of peace.* I thought the war was over. Every minute of every day, I waited for the next intercept—the one that would say a surrender was in progress. It never came, of course. The message we got wasn't written in code. It was written in bombs. *Them.* One—and then the other. Hiroshma. Nagasaki. So much for peace.

HARRY: Yes.

MARIAN: There used to be a song about Nagasaki. Do you remember?

> *(Sings.)* Hot ginger and dynamite,
> There's nothing but that at night—
> Back in Nagasaki,
> Where the fellows chew tobaccy,
> And the women wicky-wacky
> Woo!

> *(MARIAN stops suddenly.)*

Dear God—I hate who we are. I hate what we've done.

HARRY: It's all right. It's all right.

MARIAN: Nothing will ever match the barbarity of that second bomb, Harry. Seventy-five thousand dead. To teach us all—a lesson.

HARRY: I love you, Marian.

MARIAN: Yes. And I love you. For all our sins.

> *(HARRY and MARIAN exit.)*

DIANA: I was born of that moment. There in Nagasaki.

JACKMAN: *(Pause.)* Were your parents communists, Mrs. Marsden?

DIANA: That's right, Superintendent. Plotting the overthrow of everything we stand for. There isn't any hiding from your politics, is there. *(Leaving.)* Good night, Mister Jackman.

Scene Eight

(Morning. In the sunroom, MAHAVOLITCH is laying out files and papers taken from a brief-case. He wears a jogging suit with the RCMP logo on the breast-pocket.

HARRY enters the garden. At a distance, the sound of Canada geese can be heard. HARRY stops to listen. Facing front, he sights them coming as if from the back of the auditorium. As the sound increases and the geese pass overhead, HARRY shades his eyes to see them.

MAHAVOLITCH comes down to the sunroom windows from which he also watches the geese.

When the geese are directly overhead, HARRY raises his right arm in salutation. The sound of the geese is thrilling. HARRY turns all the way upstage as the geese pass over the roof of the house and the sound of them fades into the distance. Now, both men meet each other's gaze. This is brief. HARRY exits.

JACKMAN enters the sunroom. He wears shirt and tie—carries jacket, which he throws down.)

MAHAVOLITCH: You hear the geese?

JACKMAN: I heard something. Is that what it was?

MAHAVOLITCH: About fifty of them. Took me straight back to the prairie—the sound of them.

JACKMAN: You miss it—the prairies.

MAHAVOLITCH: Yeah. When I hear that kind of thing, I do.

JACKMAN: You got those files in order?

MAHAVOLITCH: Almost.

(MAHAVOLITCH returns to file selection.

JACKMAN opens the 8 x 10 envelope given to him by MICHAEL. Draws out photographs and papers.)

You think Ambassador Raymond killed this Russian?

JACKMAN: It's possible. Or maybe Mrs. Raymond.

MAHAVOLITCH: The wife could've done it?

JACKMAN: She might have. Never close a door till you're all the way through, Mahavolitch. Somebody killed the lad—*(Holds up a photo of Mischa.)*—it hardly matters who. The point is, he was killed because Harry Raymond is our ambassador. The thing we don't understand is—why did the Russians let him go?

MAHAVOLITCH: It was *them* who got in touch with the Minister? *Them* who said: "Take him home"?

JACKMAN: So we're told. But it doesn't make sense.

MAHAVOLITCH: It's a set-up. He's an agent.

JACKMAN: Could be. Make it seem he's in trouble. Set us off on the wrong track. It could be.

(He puts the photo down and picks up a file.)

MAHAVOLITCH: You trust the Minister?

JACKMAN: Michael Riordon? I'd better. He called us in on this.

MAHAVOLITCH: That doesn't mean you can trust him, sir. *(Beat.)* I never did like his politics. High-falutin' type. Left-leaning intellectual. Now, it looks like he's gonna be PM, for Christ's sake.

JACKMAN: That's right.

MAHAVOLITCH: Anti-American, too. Keeps pulling back from the Yanks. They're our allies, for Pete's sake, but he keeps pulling back. We got all their fucking deserters and all their fucking draft dodgers up here. Tolerated. Molly-coddled. There's got to be a reason. I figure it's guys like Riordon—guys like Raymond. "Come on over! We love ya!" Jesus.

JACKMAN: *(Amused.)* Someone should hire you as a border guard. Okay—let's get on with the business at hand. Potent stuff, this.

(JACKMAN hands photographs over.)

MAHAVOLITCH: *(Beaming.)* Phew! Yeah! Po—tent!

JACKMAN: You've got it.

(They become relatively immobile.

MARIAN enters the garden and stands looking down from the jutting edge. One hand is fisted.)

DIANA: *(Off.)* Mother?

(MARIAN does not react. She might as well be deaf.

DIANA comes along one of the walkways.)

You have this knack for disappearing.

MARIAN: I'm right here.

DIANA: Aren't you going to eat any breakfast?

MARIAN: I've already had lunch.

DIANA: You can't have, mother. It's nine in the morning.

MARIAN: Is it really?

DIANA: Yes. What's that in your hand?

MARIAN: Nothing.

DIANA: *(Laughs.)* Well—you seem to have a fairly tight grip on *nothing,* mother. Show me what it is.

MARIAN: *(Turning away.)* No. *(Pockets hand.)*

DIANA: All right. *(Beat.)* What are you staring at down there?

MARIAN: People. Walking under the trees. *(Suddenly yells.)* Get out from under my trees!

DIANA: Mother—for heaven's sake. You mustn't yell at people. It's rude.

  (She looks over edge.)

I don't see anyone.

MARIAN: They left.

DIANA: Oh. Well.

MARIAN: If you want to get people out of your life, Diana—yell at them.

  (Turns around and yells at house.)

Get out of my life!

  (JACKMAN and MAHAVOLITCH look up. MAHAVOLITCH crosses to windows.)

JACKMAN: Who's yelling?

MAHAVOLITCH: It's her—out in the garden.

JACKMAN: The wife?

MAHAVOLITCH: Yeah. *(Smiles.)* She's really wacky, isn't she.

JACKMAN: *(Joining him.)* No. She's really scared. *(Beat.)* I kind of like the other one. The daughter.

MAHAVOLITCH: *(Leering.)* Yeah?

JACKMAN: Yes.

MAHAVOLITCH: You better watch it, Superintendent.

JACKMAN: I know what I'm doing.

MAHAVOLITCH: Oh, sure. When it comes to women, we all know what we're doing.

DIANA: Undo your hand, mother. It's bleeding.

MARIAN: Is it?

DIANA: Yes.

(DIANA comes round and sits beside MARIAN. She forces the fist open.)

Good Lord. It's full of gravel ...

(She tips the gravel onto the ground and gets out a handkerchief.)

MARIAN: I was looking for round, smooth stones. There weren't any.

DIANA: Oh, mother ...

MARIAN: *(Withdraws hand.)* It doesn't hurt. Leave it alone.

(She wraps DIANA's handkerchief around it.)

DIANA: You should come in the house and let me wash it.

MARIAN: No. I will not go back in that house.

DIANA: All right. I'll go. I'll get some disinfectant.

(DIANA exits.

MARIAN reaches down and gathers up some of the gravel. She stares at it.)

MARIAN: *(Speaking the words.)* Back in Nagasaki—where the fellows chew tobaccy—and the women wicky-wacky—woo ...

(She lays down a single piece of gravel.)

There. *(Beat.)* Someone else's move.

(Music: Flute—Japanese.

HARRY enters the sunroom.)

HARRY: Gentlemen. Forgive me. I'm late.

Scene Nine

(Morning. To one side, a table and two chairs in the Riordon household. MICHAEL seated, reading newspapers. JULIET checking her guest list. Coffee cups.)

MICHAEL: *(Reading.)* FBI agents—this is the Washington Post—have established that the Watergate bugging incident stemmed from a massive campaign of political spying and sabotage conducted on behalf of President Nixon's re-election ...

JULIET: Fascinating. But anything of interest?

MICHAEL: No.

(He throws the Washington Post aside and picks up the New York Times.)

JULIET: Have you read the Canadian papers yet?

MICHAEL: I read them second.

JULIET: I should have thought this morning you would have read them first.

MICHAEL: Why?

JULIET: Our friends, Michael. Our friends.

> *(Lights rise on MARIAN in her garden—still playing one-handed Go with stones on bench.)*

MICHAEL: That won't be in the papers.

JULIET: Oh?

MICHAEL: Press blackout.

JULIET: At whose instigation? Yours?

MICHAEL: That's right.

JULIET: Don't you have to check that sort of thing through Cabinet?

MICHAEL: Sometimes.

JULIET: What about the PM?

MICHAEL: The PM is too ill to deal with this.

> *(MARIAN places a stone.)*

JULIET: You mean you haven't even told him?

MICHAEL: Juliet—I know what I'm doing.

> *(MARIAN sets another stone in place.)*

JULIET: Are you telling me no one knows he's here—in Ottawa? My god, Michael. You scare the hell out of me.

MICHAEL: Nonsense.

JULIET: Don't talk to me that way. I'm on your side.

MICHAEL: Then abide by the rules.

> *(MARIAN sets down another stone.)*

JULIET: *(Shaken sits.)* You're acting on your own, aren't you. You brought them out of Russia on your own.

MICHAEL: You're conducting a one-sided conversation, Juliet.

JULIET: *(Sickened; quiet.)* You're acting on your own.

MICHAEL: Prattle.

JULIET: This is not prattle.

MICHAEL: It sounds like prattle to me.

JULIET: I *know* something.

(MICHAEL looks over the Times.)

I thought that might catch your attention.

(MICHAEL carefully folds paper, lays it aside.)

MICHAEL: Is there any more coffee?

JULIET: Help yourself.

(MICHAEL rises, pours [imaginary] coffee from a pot on an [imaginary] sideboard.)

MICHAEL: So? What is it you know?

JULIET: I know about the dead boy in the Moscow hotel.

(Pause.

(MARIAN raises her hand—about to set another stone. She waits.)

MICHAEL: *(Calmly.)* Interesting. How do you know about that?

JULIET: I'm not the only prattler in town, Mike.

MICHAEL: All right. Who was it?

JULIET: I never divulge names. *(She smiles at him.)* You told me to abide by the rules, my dear.

(MARIAN sets the stone in place.

MICHAEL returns to table, sits.

JULIET pushes at her guest list.)

Do you mind if Mary Ann Turnbull sits on your left tonight.

MICHAEL: I think you had better sit on my left tonight.

JULIET: You really do take the cake. You're afraid I'll say something.

MICHAEL: Juliet …

(MICHAEL picks up a paper and sets it aside.)

JULIET: What I heard was—this dead young man might have been Marian Raymond's lover … That's the prattle.

MICHAEL: Is it, now.

JULIET: Yes, sir.

(Pause. MICHAEL rises and walks away to a window.)

MICHAEL: Juliet … I have a confession to make.

JULIET: Yes?

MICHAEL: I want to be Prime Minister. *(He looks at her.)* Do you understand what I'm saying?

JULIET: *(Pause, looks away.)* Yes. You're saying that—because of that dead young man in Moscow—you may have to throw our friends to the wolves. *(Beat.)* Because you want to be Prime Minister.

MICHAEL: Rule number one, Juliet: *one does what must be done.*

> *(JULIET turns all the way away from him.*
>
> *Lights begin to fade.*
>
> *Music: Flute rises.*
>
> *MARIAN sets the final stone in its place.)*

Scene Ten

> *(Sunroom. Noon. MAHAVOLITCH is acting as feeder for JACKMAN, handing him various pieces of paper as JACKMAN speaks.*
>
> *HARRY is in a contained mode, showing little reaction to the questions—courteous, but reserved. Not cordial, but without hostility.)*

JACKMAN: Ambassador, were you ever associated with the Institute of Pacific Relations?

HARRY: Yes. Some years ago.

JACKMAN: Did you ever write for a magazine called *Amerasia*?

HARRY: Yes. I was once considered something of an expert on the subject of Japanese culture. I served there after the war. I'd been assigned to work with General MacArthur. He was a sort of *king.* Not yet an *emperor,* if you get my drift ...

> *(MAHAVOLITCH watches him, narrow-eyed.)*

JACKMAN: You worked with a fellow Canadian there ... *(Pretends to look for name.)* a man called ... Norman.

HARRY: Herbert Norman. That's right. He was my boss. Technically, I'd been assigned to him—but his work was with General MacArthur. *(Beat.)* Superintendent—

JACKMAN: *(Cutting through.)* Herbert Norman was also an expert on Japan?

HARRY: Yes. He was *the* expert. He was born there. Of missionary parents.

JACKMAN: Your parents died ...? A car accident?

HARRY: Yes. When I was a child. An uncle raised me. My father's brother. *(Beat.)* Superintendent—it was my understanding I was here to talk about a death in Moscow.

JACKMAN: This is about a death in Moscow.

> *(He snaps his fingers and accepts next file from MAHAVOLITCH.)*

You were a student at Cambridge university?

HARRY: Yes. Kindness of my uncle. It had been my father's ambition for me.

JACKMAN: *(From list.)* And your fellow students there were Donald Maclean—Guy Burgess—and Herbert Norman?

HARRY: Yes.

JACKMAN: Over the years, you and Ambassador Norman seem to have bumped into one another rather a lot. Clearly, you shared a number of interests. Would you care to elaborate?

HARRY: I've already told you—Herbert Norman was a revered Japanese scholar. I made some minor contributions on the subject. We often spoke of things Japanese.

JACKMAN: Nothing else?

HARRY: No. Nothing else.

JACKMAN: What about communist ideology?

HARRY: Stop this! Herbert Norman was not a Communist. That has been proved conclusively. Period. End of story.

JACKMAN: And you?

HARRY: There is no reason to doubt my loyalty, Superintendent.

JACKMAN: That sounds good, Ambassador. But—loyalty to what?

HARRY: My country.

JACKMAN: Well—if you say so …

HARRY: *(Losing temper.)* I *know* so, Superintendent. *And so do you. (Cools.)* Look. Get to the point. I want to know why I am here. And my wife. And my daughter. You still have told me absolutely nothing about that young man in Moscow.

JACKMAN: Okay. The point. *(Brown envelope.)* In here, there are photographs. *(Offers envelope.)* Look at them.

HARRY: No.

> *(HARRY, clearly alarmed, turns away. JACKMAN removes photographs and offers them.)*

JACKMAN: Look at them!

HARRY: No.

JACKMAN: Ambassador Raymond—these photographs may not be pretty. They may not be uplifting. They sure as hell are not pleasant. But they are *evidence*.

HARRY: I'm sorry. I can't ... I cannot look at him dead.

JACKMAN: *(Pause.)* Who says he's dead?

HARRY: He was murdered. The Minister said so ... a hotel room in Moscow ...

JACKMAN: Well—these may show a hotel room in Moscow, Ambassador, but ... *(He looks at pictures.)* the boy in here sure ain't dead. *(Beat.)* I could show them to your wife. See what she has to say ...

>   *(HARRY sits down.)*

Maybe it would help if you spoke to her. Tell her what we have here.

HARRY: *(Long pause.)* Yes. I will speak to her. But I will not look at those photographs. I would rather be blind.

JACKMAN: Suit yourself.

HARRY: Thank you. May I go now?

JACKMAN: Yes, sir.

>   *(HARRY stands up. He is a bit lost. Turns the wrong way. JACKMAN points out the door. HARRY exits.)*

>   *(Calling after him.)* We will want to continue, Ambassador, this afternoon.

>   *(JACKMAN hands MAHAVOLITCH photographs.)*

Put these back in the envelope.

>   *(As he does this, MAHAVOLITCH turns one of the photographs sideways—and then upside down—and smiles.*
>
>   *Lights fade.*
>
>   *Music: Flute.)*

Scene Eleven

>   *(The garden.*
>
>   *Music: Flute continues.*
>
>   *HARRY enters. He walks to the jutting edge and looks at the sky. He is afraid to look down.)*

HARRY: Mischa Andreevitch Bugarin … *(Looks front.)*

> *(MARIAN enters the garden, lost.*
>
> *DIANA enters. She crosses to the bench and, stooping behind it, begins to gather up Marian's stones.)*

… nineteen years old when he died …

> *(MARIAN gets out her cigarettes.)*

DIANA: Everybody dies, father.

HARRY: Yes.

> *(MARIAN lights her cigarette.)*

But everybody isn't killed.

DIANA: *(Looks at him.)* Is that why you're here? They think it was you.

HARRY: That's right. Me.

> *(MARIAN coughs—quietly.)*

DIANA: *(Having waited.)* Was it you? *(Beat.)* Daddy?

> *(DIANA looks at MARIAN.)*

Mother? He was your friend. Who *was* he? Mischa?

HARRY: He was my lover, Diana.

> *(Music stops abruptly, mid-note.*
>
> *Nobody moves.*
>
> *Lights fade to black.*
>
> *End of Act One.)*

Act Two

Scene One

(Music: Piano. The music is vaguely "cocktail lounge"—the sort of thing that might be played as people gather for a party.

HARRY is seated on the garden bench. He now wears a tweed jacket.

MARIAN is seated in profile to the audience on one of the upper levels. She wears a Japanese kimono as a bath-robe. A small table contains a mirror and some make-up. A cigarette burns in an ashtray. She is trying to locate the person she can recognize as her "self." As she begins, there is nothing on her face but matte. She will draw on the rest. From time to time, she pauses to look at herself—and to drink.

On another of the levels, JULIET and MICHAEL prepare for their party. MICHAEL, who will end up in tuxedo/black tie, is dressed but for shirt buttons, tie and jacket. JULIET is dressed, but fixing hair.)

JULIET: How long have we been doing this ...?

MICHAEL: Since we began, I guess. 1943. Santiago—Chile.

JULIET: Our first posting. Dear me ... we were children.

MICHAEL: Well—hardly.

JULIET: We were very, very green, Mike. We knew nothing ...

MICHAEL: *(Pleasantly.)* Speak for yourself.

JULIET: I never speak for myself, my darling. I always speak for you.

MICHAEL: I was legal counsel, then. I liked that job.

JULIET: Yes. And weren't those the days. The war and everything ...

MICHAEL: *(Cannot manage cufflinks.)* Can you …?

> *(JULIET attaches links.)*

JULIET: Some of it was screamingly funny. Remember? Chile was non-combatant. Neutral. And whenever the Ambassador's wife gave a dinner party, all the warring factions would have to be kept at a strategic distance from one another … all those pompous delegations in uniform …

MICHAEL: The Germans. Yes. The Italians …

JULIET: The Spaniards. All the fascists … *(Completes cufflinks.)* There you go. And of course, being in uniform, they came to the dinner parties armed to the teeth! The Ambassador's wife said this was intolerable. She refused to allow the wearing of firearms at her table. You remember this?

MICHAEL: No. I remember the men being in uniform—but that's all.

JULIET: What she did was—oh, it was wonderful—she set out squares of white lace beside all the wine glasses—and the Germans, the Italians, the Spaniards were all required to lay their pistols down on these … *(Laughs.)* gun-doilies. That's what we called them. Gun-doilies, my darling! Talk about diplomacy!

MICHAEL: Tie, please.

> *(JULIET straightens his tie. He starts to move for his jacket. She pulls him back—using his suspenders.)*

JULIET: Michael …

MICHAEL: Yes?

JULIET: Don't harm them. Our friends.

MICHAEL: Our guests are about to arrive.

JULIET: Michael—please.

MICHAEL: *(Frees himself.)* Leave our friends to me, Juliet. Don't interfere.

JULIET: What if it was us—in trouble?

MICHAEL: *(Jacket.)* It's not us. It's them.

JULIET: *Us*—and *them.* That sounds familiar, somehow.

MICHAEL: It's time, Juliet. Our guests … *(Exits.)*

JULIET: *(Pause.)* It's time, Juliet. Our guests. Yes. And how will I get them to put their guns on the table … *(Exits.)*

(Their lights fade.

Music: The piano alters.

DIANA enters the upper platform where MARIAN sits. MARIAN sees her in the mirror.)

MARIAN: Get out.

(DIANA exits.

Lights fade on MARIAN.)

Scene Two

(DIANA goes to the sunroom via steps and walkways.

A dog barks off in the distance.

MAHAVOLITCH, in running shorts and sweat shirt, enters the garden.)

MAHAVOLITCH: Hi, there.

HARRY: Hello.

MAHAVOLITCH: Great evening for it.

HARRY: Great evening for what?

MAHAVOLITCH: Running.

HARRY: Oh, yes.

(DIANA, in the sunroom, pours a drink for herself.)

MAHAVOLITCH: You ever?

HARRY: Ever what?

MAHAVOLITCH: Get out there and pound the pavement.

HARRY: No.

MAHAVOLITCH: Nothing like it. Might do you some good. You never know.

HARRY: Somehow, I doubt it. I'm an old man, Corporal. Old men don't run.

MAHAVOLITCH: My old man did.

HARRY: Bravo.

MAHAVOLITCH: I'm from Regina. My old man used to park us on the prairie and both of us would get out and run. Ten miles and more.

HARRY: I envy you.

MAHAVOLITCH: Yeah?

HARRY: Yes. The distance.

DIANA: Father? *(To MAHAVOLITCH.)* Good evening.

MAHAVOLITCH: Hi.

DIANA: *(Coming down steps.)* Do you think we could be alone for a moment, Corporal?

MAHAVOLITCH: Sure. I got to go and shower, anyway.

DIANA: He won't run away, I promise.

HARRY: You don't have to promise, Diana. I've already told him I'm too old. And not inclined.

MAHAVOLITCH: See you.

HARRY: Yes. Indeed.

> *(MAHAVOLITCH exits.)*

Scene Three

> *(DIANA crosses downstage.)*

HARRY: Before you speak, Diana, I have something to say.

DIANA: No. It's my turn to speak.

HARRY: What? Your summation. You haven't heard the whole case.

DIANA: This is not a "case," father.

HARRY: You could have fooled me. You're being so aggressive, I'm surprised you're not wearing your gown. *(Rises.)*

DIANA: You want me to get it? Would it make you feel more secure? That way, at least, you could identify me.

> *(HARRY crosses to the jutting edge.)*

That's right—walk away. I still recognize defensive behaviour when I see it. That I do recognize—but not much else.

HARRY: What does that mean?

DIANA: *(Letting it out.)* It means I don't know who you are!

HARRY: I'm your father. How do you do.

DIANA: Don't you dare demean the way I feel.

HARRY: *(Angry.)* I love you, Diana.

DIANA: Tell me all about it!

HARRY: I love you. I love you. That is all I have to say.

DIANA: Is that what you said to mother?

HARRY: You don't understand.

DIANA: Damn right I don't. Damn bloody right I don't. How can I? What am I supposed to understand? That all my life you've lied about who you are? That everything you said and did was a lie? *(Beat.)* God in heaven, father—I don't care *what* you are. But I have a right to know *who* you are—who my father *is*.

I cannot begin to describe how I have admired you all these years. How profoundly I have admired you. I looked upon you—I told that man in there—I told him that I looked upon you with wonder. *Wonder*, father. *God damn it.*

  (Almost loses control, but regains it.)

It was always the thought of you, father, that saved me when other men battered me with their lies and self-deception. But I always knew they were lying. I always knew they deceived themselves about who they were and how righteous they were! They were bastards—every one of them! Every one of them *lied*. And they were so full of pride and self that most of the time they didn't even know they were lying.

Men are like that. Men are like that—but not you. Not you. You were whole. You were a whole man ... true, above all other things, to yourself. I knew who you were. And now you want me to understand ... I am given to understand ... I am supposed to understand that I don't know you. All of a sudden—bam! An instant stranger. What am I going to do with this information, father? Not that you're queer— who gives a damn! But that you lied. You lied. You lied, like all the rest—and my problem is, I don't know where the lie begins—and I don't know where it ends.

HARRY: It ends where it began. There is nothing more to say. *(Beat.)* How the hell am I supposed to talk about this? What can I possibly tell you? This is not something that happened to you, Diana. It happened to me. And to your mother. *We* are paying for this—not you. Come down from your great, hurt place and the "privilege" of pain. It is unbecoming to you.

DIANA: Somehow, that doesn't bother me, father. I still want to know who you are.

HARRY: I have nothing to say.

DIANA: What? Still in hiding?

HARRY: Silence is not a hiding place, Diana.

DIANA: It seems to have provided a pretty damn good hiding place for you.

HARRY: I am not in hiding. I am here. Right here—standing in front of you. *Me.*

> *(JACKMAN comes onto a walkway, more in shadow than in light.)*

If you can't see me, Diana—tough.

> *(MARIAN enters the sunroom, still wearing her robe. She pours herself a drink.)*

You say "who gives a damn" if I'm homosexual. *I do.* My *work* does. My *government* does. *Do not be a homosexual. Do not be a homosexual. Do not be that. Be anything—but do not be a homosexual.*

> *(JACKMAN shifts his position slightly.)*

Tell me something, Diana. I'd be fascinated to know how you might defend me if the subject of who I really am were ever brought to trial. Eh? How would you do that?

> *(No answer.)*

May I remind you *that silence is not a hiding place?*

DIANA: I can't answer the question.

HARRY: Yes, you can. Try.

> *(DIANA turns away.)*

Frightened, aren't you? Scared. *God knows what else is hidden in here.* Is that it? *Me—the immoral seducer of hundreds—maybe thousands of young men? Me—the pervert? Me—the murderer? (Beat.)* Damn right, Diana. You don't know me. But not because I lied. You don't know me because you do not want to know *me.* You want to know a stranger. An invention.

DIANA: I did not invent you, father. You invented yourself: *Harry Raymond—straight as a die!*

HARRY: *(Pause.)* Feeling better?

DIANA: Yes!

HARRY: Interesting, isn't it? You've just revealed a prejudice you didn't know you had. *(Beat.)* Put it this way, Diana—say I had been out there where you and everyone else could see me. What would you have done with that? You, with your liberal ideals—how would you have explained me to your friends? Your lovers—your husbands? All those righteous bastards you consorted with. How would you have done that?

DIANA: *(Quiet.)* I could have said ... I would have ... said ... *(Stops.)*

HARRY: *(Quiet.)* There you are, then.

DIANA: Yes. Here I am. I'm sorry, father.

HARRY: How dare you be *sorry.* You—with your refusal to let people
be. Why do you think they lied to you—all those men you hate? Your
boyfriends, your lovers, your husbands—why do you think they lied?
They lied because you would not let them be who they were. They
had to lie in order to win you.

DIANA: I'm not a prize, father.

HARRY: You're damn right you're not.

DIANA: Oh, please—why are we doing this?

HARRY: We're doing this because this is how people survive. We kill
whatever stands in our way.

DIANA: You don't believe that.

HARRY: I killed what stood in my way, Diana. Stone dead.

> *(JACKMAN shifts again.)*

DIANA: *(Pause.)* Are you telling me you killed this boy?

> *(HARRY walks away from her.)*

Are you telling me you killed him?

HARRY: Do you never listen? I'm telling you I killed my self.

> *(MARIAN lights a cigarette.)*

DIANA: But ... then, why Mischa?

HARRY: Mischa ... *(Pause.)*

> *(MAHAVOLITCH walks onto one of the upper levels. He wears a
> towel around his waist—and is otherwise naked.*
>
> *HARRY speaks with genuine remembered affection, touched with
> the knowledge of Mischa's betrayal.)*

Mischa. Yes. *(Beat.)* When I saw him first, it was like those meetings
you have in dreams, when a stranger greets you and you recognize
him instantly. *You, is it? I've been waiting for you.* I was his Lazarus,
he was my miracle worker. Rise up and walk. Rejoin the living ...

> *(MAHAVOLITCH removes the towel and dries his torso.)*

The living look so—beautiful, Diana. So unbearably beautiful—to
the dead.

DIANA: *(Pause.)* Were you lovers for very long?

HARRY: No. Less than a year. A matter of months. Weeks. He was just very suddenly … *there.* We were in the south, your mother and I. She was already ill, probably had been for quite a while. But with Alzheimer's—who knows when it begins? She was tense. Tired. She kept forgetting where we were. Total disorientation. She saw the palm trees and thought we were in Cairo.

DIANA: And where were you?

HARRY: Yalta. It sits on a series of hills above the Black Sea. It is where all good Russians go to recuperate. There are baths there—the waters. Which is how we met. In the baths. He walked right up to me and spoke his name. Naked. I was lost. There was nothing I could do. My defenses—the whole castle—fell.

> *(MAHAVOLITCH throws the towel to one side and begins to dress.)*

DIANA: Why was he killed—if he was only your friend?

> *(HARRY does not answer this.*
>
> *JACKMAN moves slowly along the walkway.)*

He died in Moscow. Was it you who brought him back there? From Yalta.

HARRY: No. I would not have dared do that. He came there on his own. It was a shock, I'm here to tell you, when he walked into my office one day and said: "Here I am." I met him on my holidays—he came to me on his. He was a student. Of acting. He wanted to be an actor.

> *(MARIAN comes to the top of the sunroom steps.)*

MARIAN: *(As if to herself.)* My goodness! It's just like summer—an evening in August. Look at the moon. And everything is so still.

DIANA: What about mother, father?

HARRY: What about her?

DIANA: She's so distracted. Almost like someone adrift. Isn't there something I can do?

HARRY: I thought you would never ask, Diana. *(Smiles.)* Yes. You can get us something to eat.

DIANA: Mother? Are you hungry?

MARIAN: There's some chicken à la king in there. In cans.

DIANA: I'll go and heat it up.

(DIANA crosses the garden to the steps, seeing JACKMAN as she goes.)

Don't you ever go away?

HARRY: He can't go away, Diana. He's a part of us, now. The watcher— watching. The listener—listening, no doubt. Good evening, Superintendent.

JACKMAN: *(Turning.)* Yes, sir. Very pleasant.

HARRY: That's right. "Very pleasant." Saw nothing. Blind. Heard nothing. Deaf.

(MARIAN comes down and sits on the bench with her drink.

DIANA exits through the sunroom.)

Have you eaten, Superintendent?

JACKMAN: Thank you. It's all arranged. We have a pizza coming in.

HARRY: With or without anchovies?

JACKMAN: With, Ambassador. *With.* Those of us from by the sea can't do without our salt.

HARRY: *(Moving towards the sunroom.)* I take it you will want me in the morning.

JACKMAN: No, sir. I will want you this evening—once you've dined.

(HARRY goes up into the sunroom, turning for a brief look at MARIAN. Then he goes to pour himself a drink.)

Scene Four

(The garden. Lights come on in the sunroom as HARRY moves from lamp to lamp. The moonlight is intense.

JACKMAN moves down into the garden.

Music: from somewhere in the house, a radio can be heard. A record is being played of a sentimental song.)

MARIAN: Have you come to ask me to dance?

JACKMAN: I don't think so, ma'am.

MARIAN: Why not? You've been dancing all day with my husband.

JACKMAN: Very well said, ma'am.

MARIAN: *(Looks at him.)* You're some kind of killer, aren't you.

JACKMAN: Oh—I don't think that's quite fair. I have my job to do. Same as you.

MARIAN: I have no job.

JACKMAN: Oh, I think you do, ma'am. Ambassador's wife—all that entails. You've had a long career of it, haven't you?

MARIAN: Long enough. How old do you think I am?

JACKMAN: It's not your age I'm interested in, Mrs. Raymond. It's your experience. What you remember.

MARIAN: I don't remember anything. Nothing. I can't seem to pull my mind into … *(Drifts.)*

JACKMAN: *(Pause.)* Focus, ma'am?

MARIAN: What?

JACKMAN: Your mind. You were saying …

MARIAN: I forget.

> *(She rises, crosses away from him.)*

JACKMAN: I was sort of hoping you could help me with some answers. The Minister, for instance. Mister Riordon. Is it true that he knew your husband when they were both young men?

MARIAN: Yes.

JACKMAN: Where might that have been, Mrs. Raymond?

MARIAN: Somewhere. I don't know.

JACKMAN: Was it the war?

MARIAN: The war?

JACKMAN: The Second World War.

MARIAN: I was a cipher clerk.

JACKMAN: Yes. But your husband—your husband and Mister Riordon …

MARIAN: They are not lovers, Superintendent.

JACKMAN: No, ma'am. I realize that. *(Gathers patience.)* Was it Michael Riordon who was Minister when your husband received his posting to Moscow?

MARIAN: The posting came through the mail.

> *(Doorbell rings—off.)*

Reinforcements have arrived. Yours, I believe.

> *(Inside, the radio is shut off.)*

What a pity. No more dancing.

JACKMAN: Yes, ma'am. thank you. *(Realizes she has thwarted him.)* You dance—very well.

(MARIAN drops him a mock curtsey.)

I'm afraid I'll have to keep your husband busy for a while tonight.

MARIAN: Suit yourself. He's a grown man.

(MAHAVOLITCH comes onto walkway with a pizza box.)

MAHAVOLITCH: Pizza's up.

JACKMAN: Yes.

(MAHAVOLITCH exits.)

Well, then …

MARIAN: Good evening.

JACKMAN: Good evening.

(JACKMAN exits into the sunroom.)

MARIAN: *(No emotion.)* Bastard.

(DIANA enters.)

DIANA: Mother? Food.

(MARIAN waves her off. She drinks.

Lights change.

In the sunroom, MAHAVOLITCH has joined HARRY and JACKMAN.)

JACKMAN: In 1936 you were a student at Cambridge University.

HARRY: Yes. At Trinity College.

MAHAVOLITCH: Pizza?

JACKMAN: Thanks. Around that time, you were friendly with a young man named Francis Oliver.

HARRY: That's right.

JACKMAN: This Francis Oliver was a Socialist. Is that correct?

MARIAN: Don't.

HARRY: Actually, he called himself a Communist.

MARIAN: Don't.

JACKMAN: *(Checks file.)* Francis Oliver was a good deal younger than you, was he not?

HARRY: Yes.

JACKMAN: What you might call a boy.

MARIAN: Make them stop. *(Yells.)* Stop! Don't!

DIANA: *(Crossing to her.)* Mother—come in. *Now.*

MARIAN: *(Subsides.)* Yes.

> *(They begin to cross to walkway exit as the garden light fades.)*

They don't know what they're doing to him. They don't understand what they're doing. *(Turning back.)* Stop!

> *(MARIAN and DIANA exit.)*

Scene Five

(Sunroom.)

JACKMAN: *(Eating pizza.)* It says here Francis Oliver was a well-known organizer of political meetings and *(Eating makes next words unintelligible.)* left-wing demonstrations …

HARRY: Meetings and …?

JACKMAN: *(Clearly.)* Left-wing demonstrations.

HARRY: Well—he was a Socialist, wasn't he. He was also a poet … That's what I remember. The poet.

JACKMAN: His mother was well-known, too. Dorothy Oliver wrote for the left-wing press. Then there was his great-grandfather, Charles Darwin …

HARRY: *(Amused.)* Another radical … Quite a family.

JACKMAN: *(Reading from file.)* In 1937, Oliver left the Young Communist League …

HARRY: *(Waving his handkerchief.)* Hurray!

JACKMAN: … in order to become a full-fledged member of the Communist Party.

HARRY: Not "hurray." Presumably.

JACKMAN: Right you are, Mister Raymond. No "hurray" this time. Because it says here that in March of 1937—you, too, became a full-fledged Communist.

HARRY: Does it really? Well. What a pity.

MAHAVOLITCH: *(Referring to file.)* Francis Oliver was quite a boy—according to this.

HARRY: Yes. He was.

MAHAVOLITCH: He had a lot of followers, it says here—you among them.

HARRY: I was his best friend. *(Pause.)* I adored him.

MAHAVOLITCH: Adored?

HARRY: Yes.

(JACKMAN and MAHAVOLITCH exchange a look.)

MAHAVOLITCH: Isn't that a strange thing to say about another man, Mister Raymond?

HARRY: I don't think so. I adored my uncle, too. And my uncle—by the way—was not a Communist.

JACKMAN: *(Checks paper.)* He was a philosopher.

HARRY: He taught philosophy, Superintendent. There's a difference.

MAHAVOLITCH: Isn't communism a philosophy?

HARRY: It's a theory.

JACKMAN: There's a difference. *(Smiles.)* Now—about Francis Oliver. He was instrumental, then, in drawing you into the Communist Party?

HARRY: Francis Oliver could have drawn an angel into hell.

JACKMAN: But he drew *you* into the Communist Party.

HARRY: I went freely, Superintendent—happily, of my own accord. I approved of Marx. *Das Kapital* was a call to arms. I was young. It was a volatile world, back then, politically. Unlike today, the enemies of the people could be seen—identified—named. Hitler—Mussolini—Franco. Taking a stand against them seemed the only proper thing to do, for a young man with ideals.

(JACKMAN refers to MAHAVOLITCH's file.)

JACKMAN: It says here that in 1938, Francis Oliver went to Spain.

(HARRY turns away and walks to edge of the sunroom, facing front.)

HARRY: Yes. He did.

JACKMAN: Where he fought in the Civil War on the Loyalist side.

HARRY: That's right.

JACKMAN: The Loyalists, at that time, were receiving aid from the Soviet Union. Yes.

HARRY: Correct. The whole of the Spanish Civil War was a communist conspiracy.

MAHAVOLITCH: *(To JACKMAN.)* Who won?

HARRY: You did.

(Music: Guitar. A Spanish sequence of chords.)

MAHAVOLITCH: What happened? To Francis Oliver?

JACKMAN: *(Without emotion.)* He was killed. At Barcelona.

HARRY: December—1938. He was twenty years old *(Pause.)* He died. I did not. He is dead. I am still here.

(The lights fade

Music: Concludes.

MARIAN enters upper level—still wearing robe. She prepares for bed. She carries drink and the inevitable cigarettes and lighter.

In the sunroom, JACKMAN and MAHAVOLITCH are clearing files, etc.

HARRY crosses to the drinks tray and takes up a bottle and glass. He holds up the scotch.)

Sleep in a bottle. Goodnight, gentlemen.

JACKMAN: Goodnight, Ambassador. In the morning ...

HARRY: Yes, yes. In the morning.

(HARRY exits sunroom and begins to make his way via steps and walkways to the upper level where MARIAN awaits him.)

Scene Six

MAHAVOLITCH: Who the hell was this guy—Francis Oliver?

JACKMAN: An idealist.

MAHAVOLITCH: So?

JACKMAN: So—he died for what he believed in. Don't knock it. Let me show you something.

(JACKMAN retrieves envelope of photographs. He removes some photographs and a second envelope from the first. He takes a single photo from the second envelope.)

I've been saving this. Perhaps you'd better look at it now.

(MAHAVOLITCH looks.

HARRY, partway to his destination, pauses, out of breath.)

MAHAVOLITCH: *(Obviously sickened.)* Holy shit ... I don't want to see that.

JACKMAN: Hold it in your hand, Corporal. It's only a photograph.

(MAHAVOLITCH, reluctant, does so.)

There. A boy. A mere boy. What? Nineteen? Twenty?

(MAHAVOLITCH lets photograph droop.)

Look at it!

(MAHAVOLITCH does so.)

Not just at the picture, Corporal. Look at *him.* A portrait of commitment.

MAHAVOLITCH: He's dead.

JACKMAN: *(Harshly.)* Of course he's dead.

MAHAVOLITCH: *(Pause.)* Why?

JACKMAN: He believed. He was committed—one hundred per cent.

MAHAVOLITCH: You said he wanted to be an actor.

(HARRY moves on.)

JACKMAN: He was an actor. And a good one.

MAHAVOLITCH: You mean—he wasn't a homosexual? He was a plant, pretending to be queer?

JACKMAN: Sound familiar?

MAHAVOLITCH: It was all a scam. The usual.

JACKMAN: You've got it. Entrapment. Blackmail. They already had our friend Raymond's ideological sympathies. Once they had the photographs—he was all theirs.

MAHAVOLITCH: But he's our bloody ambassador!

(JACKMAN ignores this and takes photographs from MAHAVOLITCH.)

JACKMAN: It worries me, though—the *double whammy* aspect—the need to blackmail a man whose political history ... *(Looking at photographs.)* There's something still hidden in all of this. The dead boy—Mischa—why did he have to be killed? Just for a minute, I mean, assume the KGB did it.

MAHAVOLITCH: Kill their own person?

JACKMAN: Could be.

MAHAVOLITCH: But why?

JACKMAN: I don't know. It bothers me ...

MAHAVOLITCH: You don't think Raymond did it to protect himself?

JACKMAN: Could be. It could also have been her—for the same reason.

MAHAVOLITCH: The crazy lady?

JACKMAN: Not crazy, Mahavolitch.

MAHAVOLITCH: I know, I know. She has … I forget.

JACKMAN: Alzheimer's disease.

MAHAVOLITCH: Yeah—affects the memory.

JACKMAN: Of course, in this instance, it may well have another name …

MAHAVOLITCH: Oh? What?

JACKMAN: *Loyalty.* Also affects the memory. Muddles the past. Forgets …

MAHAVOLITCH: You mean she's lying … pretending to be sick, just to protect *him?*

JACKMAN: Somebody killed this kid. Somebody had a reason. It's the reason that counts. Not who did it—but why. You learn that, once you've had to do it. Cold-blooded … *(Beat.)* I take it you have never killed, Mahavolitch.

> *(HARRY enters the bedroom level.*
>
> *MARIAN puts out her hand in HARRY's direction.)*

MAHAVOLITCH: Not yet. No.

JACKMAN: You will. One day. I had to. Once.

> *(JACKMAN replaces the photograph in the envelope.*
>
> *HARRY pours two drinks.)*

MAHAVOLITCH: Yeah?

JACKMAN: Yeah.

> *(He gathers his topcoat from one of the chairs and puts it on.)*

MAHAVOLITCH: You're going out?

JACKMAN: I'm going out.

MAHAVOLITCH: Am I going with you?

JACKMAN: Of course not. Our guests.

> *(JACKMAN starts to exit.)*

MAHAVOLITCH: Where are you going?

JACKMAN: To the boss. On a hunch. *(Exits.)*

(MAHAVOLITCH picks up the envelope and looks at it. He takes out the photograph of Mischa dead and forces himself to look at it. The lights fade on MAHAVOLITCH.)

Scene Seven

(Lights rise on upper level area of Harry and Marian's bedroom. MARIAN seated; HARRY standing.)

HARRY: It's all falling apart. It's all caving in ...

MARIAN: Things fall apart. The centre will not hold ... What happens to us now?

HARRY: We wait.

MARIAN: What for?

HARRY: Clarification.

MARIAN: Of what?

HARRY: Of how the universe intends to unfold. In the meantime, *(Raises glass in toast.)* we hold. *(Drinks.)*

MARIAN: To what, Harry? Hold to what?

HARRY: Us. To ourselves

MARIAN: I don't know who I am, any more.

HARRY: *(As if he had not heard.)* We're not alone. We still have Mike.

(MARIAN stares at him—afraid.

HARRY turns and looks at her.)

Why the expression?

MARIAN: Nothing. Just something you said.

HARRY: What?

MARIAN: I don't know—just something you said. More, please ...

(MARIAN holds out her glass. HARRY pours them each a drink. MARIAN gives HARRY a radiant smile.

Music: Guitar—Spanish melody.

Their lights fade.)

Scene Eight

(Antechamber, Riordon household. A closed oak door. MICHAEL and JACKMAN. MICHAEL is in evening dress.

Music: Piano—plus some chatter beyond the door.)

MICHAEL: Well? What's so bloody urgent?

JACKMAN: We're making progress, sir. Some.

MICHAEL: You've shown him the photographs?

JACKMAN: I ... tried.

MICHAEL: What do you mean?

JACKMAN: He refused to look at them.

MICHAEL: Have you told him what the compromising photographs reveal?

JACKMAN: *(With humour.)* He seems to know, sir.

> *(Sound: There is a burst of party noise—someone has told a joke. Laughter beyond closed door.)*

MICHAEL: What do you make of him, Superintendent? Do you think he did this dreadful thing?

JACKMAN: Which "dreadful thing" is that, sir?

MICHAEL: Why, the killing, of course. The boy. What else could I mean?

JACKMAN: The photographs—the blackmail. His homosexuality, sir. That's pretty dreadful in itself—given his high position.

MICHAEL: *(Wary.)* You think so, do you.

JACKMAN: I know so. What was he doing there, sir? In Moscow, of all places—an ambassador with homosexual tendencies. Sort of like tempting fate, isn't it—someone queer in such a sensitive position— when we all know they entrap the gay boys, drop of a hat. The easiest mark in town. Isn't that the way it goes?

MICHAEL: I was not aware of Ambassador Raymond's proclivities, Superintendent. If I had been, I would hardly have placed him in jeopardy.

JACKMAN: *Him,* sir? Or the country?

MICHAEL: I beg your pardon?

JACKMAN: I'm not accusing you, Minister. It's just—you must be aware the Americans are very hot on this subject. They've been on to us through the CIA, insisting the RCMP root out and remove all homosexuals from sensitive areas. The fact is, they would like to see us get rid of all homosexuals in government, period.

MICHAEL: Not much hope of that.

JACKMAN: *(With humour.)* If we could clear them out of External, the CIA would be satisfied.

MICHAEL: Would they, now.

JACKMAN: That's why I brought in Corporal Mahavolitch, sir. It's part of his unit's mandate—rooting out homosexuals. Normally, of course, we would pass whatever we find on to the Solicitor General. But in Ambassador Raymond's case—well ... You brought us in on this yourself, didn't you, sir.

MICHAEL: *(Carefully.)* Yes. I did.

JACKMAN: Well, now—I haven't asked why that should be, sir. Have I.

MICHAEL: *(Carefully.)* No. You haven't.

JACKMAN: And I won't. Will I. I just thought it should be said: reiterated. You and me—we have *an understanding.* Am I correct?

MICHAEL: Yes. We have an understanding. *(Pause.)* Before you go, Superintendent—I think you should know a communiqué has arrived. From Moscow.

JACKMAN: Oh?

MICHAEL: They don't want him back. The Soviets.

> *(He hands the paper to JACKMAN, who reads it as MICHAEL continues.)*

As you can see, the wording is subtle—"not at this time ... as we await developments at your end ..."

> *(JACKMAN folds the page and hands it back to MICHAEL.)*

My fear is—a bargain has already been struck—an arrangement has already been set in motion as a result of this boy's death. Clearly, time is of the essence. All we know is—a young man lies dead in Moscow—was murdered brutally—was Harry Raymond's lover, whore, whatever—and now, they "await developments" at our end.

JACKMAN: Yes, sir.

> *(Beyond the door, someone is making a humorous tribute to MICHAEL. JACKMAN turns to listen.)*

MICHAEL: So far, you tell me, nothing has been forthcoming. I want results—"Developments." And that is *your* job.

JACKMAN: Are you sure, sir?

MICHAEL: Absolutely!

JACKMAN: Are you sure the developments they refer to are all up to me? Or …

MICHAEL: Or what?

JACKMAN: It just occurred to me, sir—they could be referring to developments in there, sir. *(Off stage.)* The Prime Minister's condition—the transference of power.

MICHAEL: Thank you, Superintendent, for your brilliant insight. And now—if you will excuse me … good night.

JACKMAN: Yes, sir. Thank you, sir.

> *(JACKMAN exits.*
>
> *Lights rise on upper level area of Harry and Marian's bedroom. MARIAN seated; HARRY standing.*
>
> *Music: Guitar evokes memories of heat.)*

MARIAN: Cairo. Cool white balconies—red tile floors. And ceiling fans … Tall frosted glasses full of lemonade or …

HARRY: Pimms. I remember the Pimms. Slices of cucumber, strawberries …

MARIAN: Harry?

> *(HARRY and MARIAN exit.)*

Scene Nine

> *(Antechamber. MICHAEL alone. He steps toward exit. The party noises rise. He pauses in the light spill of the "doorway"—a silhouette, frozen. Slowly, he steps back, turns and faces front. He removes his handkerchief from trouser pocket—unfolds it—stares at it—raises it to his face—dries his forehead and, dabbing at his lips, stands again frozen—the handkerchief hanging down from his fingers.)*

JULIET: *(Off.)* Mike? Michael?

> *(MICHAEL reanimates. He straightens—and makes a show of drying the back of his neck and the palms and backs of his hands. He does all this slowly.*

JULIET enters—carrying a red rose.)

Oh, my darling—oh, my dear one! *We are on our way!* Straight to the top—where we belong. What was it Hamlet said?

MICHAEL: Hamlet said a lot of things, Juliet. Which did you have in mind?

JULIET: *The readiness is all.* Yes? The readiness is all—and we are *ready!* That whole room in there is primed to offer you the crown, Mike.

(More off stage sounds of celebration.)

Listen to them. Listen to them. And it's all for you. A triumph. Every single person we invited—every single one of them answered the call.

(Off stage music.)

Sometimes, I think what a pity it is more people aren't allowed to see how it's all made to work. The ingenuity—the artfulness—the wiliness—the subterfuge. The skill, my darling, which makes it all seem inevitable. The strategies. The machinations. Yes—the underhandedness—but oh—the finesse! We've come such a long, long way—and we're *here!*

MICHAEL: Yes. Here we are.

JULIET: Survival of the fittest—yes? We've survived it all. Unlike some … I can't get them out of my mind. Harry. Marian. It's as if they'd ridden with us all the way to the top beside us—and then fell back. Stricken. Incapable. Wounded. *(Brightens.)* You remember the four of us together? *(Laughs.)* People used to think I was having an affair with Harry …

(MICHAEL snorts.)

Don't be so smug. People also thought you were having an affair with Marian.

MICHAEL: What will they think of next?

JULIET: Oh—I don't know. *(Shows the rose.)* That I'm having an affair with the PM. *(Beat.)* The thing is—no one will ever know about people like us. We're too well hidden, our crowd. The diplomatic corps. Make a picture of it, Mike. All of us standing there together. None of our eyes revealing anything—none of our mouths betraying a trace of regret or of pain. The way we stand. The way we allow ourselves to be seen but never known. The way—in public—we *hold* ourselves. The way we hold our glasses. The way we hold our liquor. The way we hold our tongues. The way we dress. The way we present our "persons." No privacy. No private lives. No lives at all, that one can see. But always—always there to be of service. I like to believe that's what the "external" in External Affairs describes—our talent—our aptitude—our *genius* for survival. *(Beat.)* Except ...

(There is the sound of applause and laughter from beyond the door. JULIET is distracted by it.)

MICHAEL: Except ...?

JULIET: Not all of us survive.

(More applause—approving laughter.)

Were you aware that Harry Raymond once had a breakdown?

MICHAEL: Breakdown? No. When?

JULIET: In Cairo. Back in the fifties, when Harry was ambassador to Egypt. Didn't you know? Marian told me.

MICHAEL: No. I never knew about it.

JULIET: I probably shouldn't have told you. A breakdown should be private. Apparently Marian nearly lost him—that's how bad it was. Poor man.

(Off stage, some of the guests have started rhythmic clapping.)

I guess we should go back.

MICHAEL: Yes.

(The clapping increases. JULIET looks at MICHAEL and smiles.)

JULIET: It's you they want, now.

MICHAEL: Yes.

JULIET: Give me your hand, then.

(The clapping is now very loud. JULIET leads MICHAEL to the door. There is a burst of applause.)

You first!

(MICHAEL exits.

JULIET pauses—only for a moment. She hurries back to the mirror. Seeing herself, she thinks of the consequences of what is taking place. She thinks of Harry and Marian. And then she turns her back on them—and follows MICHAEL into what has now become cheering.

Party noises rise.

Music: Guitar, a chord. Then flute joins in: crossover to past.)

Scene Ten

(Upper level. HARRY and MARIAN. Light patterns alter—a suggestion of louvered shutters.

In the garden, DIANA appears, wearing her topcoat. She sits on the bench.

MARIAN is seated at her little table. She turns on a lamp)

MARIAN: *(Younger.)* Tell me what happened today, Harry.

HARRY: *(Younger.)* Everything. Nothing.

MARIAN: *(Rising.)* More of everything than nothing, I suspect. I've never seen you work so hard.

HARRY: I don't mind the work. I thrive on it.

MARIAN: You may think you thrive on it, my darling—but it's really the other way round: *work thrives on you.* You look like the walking dead.

(MARIAN crosses upstage and they both unloop the ties that have restrained a cloud of mosquito netting. The netting falls. MARIAN gathers up one end and creates a swatch, as if over a bed.)

Just when we get to be Ambassador to Egypt, the whole Middle East explodes. So tell me—what did you do today?

HARRY: The Americans have landed troops in Lebanon. I spent the whole day with Colonel Nasser—trying to rein him in.

MARIAN: Come and sit down.

HARRY: *(Sits.)* Marines in Beirut. That lovely city …

MARIAN: I know.

HARRY: All our peace-keeping efforts gone up in smoke.

MARIAN: I know.

HARRY: *(Conjuring.)* It seems I'm doomed to work in a world run by military madmen. In Japan, it was General MacArthur. Where he lived—do you remember?—there was a garden. An ancient, civilized Japanese garden. With raked sand to walk in. It was so quiet there …

MARIAN: Yes. I remember.

HARRY: MacArthur never raised his voice. Not ever. During the Korean war, in that garden, he would whisper: "My air force will cut their troops to pieces. My bombs will decimate their people. Their cities will lie in ruin …"

MARIAN: *(Whispers.)* Yes.

HARRY: All my working life, I said: no. *No.* That's why diplomacy exists. That's what it's for. *No. Don't.*

MARIAN: Yes.

HARRY: *(Beat.)* Having had your say—knowing MacArthur has not even bothered to listen—you rise to leave him and walk away across the sand. And then this man comes out—gardener—Japanese—and he rakes away your imprint. It is just as if you had never been there.

> *(MARIAN goes to her table and pours him another drink—and for herself.)*

Now—this. Another General—President Eisenhower—has sent the Marines to Beirut.

> *(MARIAN laughs.)*

It's funny?

MARIAN: No. But I just had this image of a boatload of Japanese gardeners going in after the troops to rake away their footprints.

HARRY: Oh, god. *(Suddenly weeps.)*

MARIAN: Don't, Harry. Don't. Please—please. Come to bed and rest.

HARRY: *(Rising, angry.)* I don't want to rest. I will not rest. Have I not made myself clear? Is something missing here? I have a job to do. I'm a diplomat. A peacemaker. God dammit! I want to work. I want … *(Moves away and leans on her table.)* I want—I must—I have to work.

MARIAN: Your work is killing you.

HARRY: Don't try to manoeuvre me out of the one thing I can do.

MARIAN: No one's manoeuvring you anywhere. I'm merely suggesting that you stop for a moment. Give yourself the benefit of doing something for *you*—for Harry. Pause. Breathe. Take a day off. Good Lord, you have lots of talented people on your staff—why not give them a chance? You never let anyone else do anything.

HARRY: I can't.

MARIAN: Maybe you can't. But you will.

HARRY: I must work …

MARIAN: No, Harry. Sleep. The least you can do is try. Please.

HARRY: It won't … I can't …

MARIAN: Yes, you can. Go.

(HARRY goes behind the netting. MARIAN watches after him. When he is gone, she lights a cigarette and faces front.)

(Singing to herself.) Back in Nagasaki … where the men all chew tobaccy … and the women … *(Stops.)* Harry?

(MARIAN turns and goes behind the netting.

Lights dim.)

Scene Eleven

(The garden. Morning. Sunlight. DIANA is seated on the bench, as before, but she has removed her top-coat and now lays it on the bench beside her.

MAHAVOLITCH passes her, wearing running gear. Exits.

MARIAN enters from one of the walkways. She wears a pale dress and sunglasses.

HARRY paces on the upper level.)

DIANA: How did you sleep?

MARIAN: I dreamt. I think I dreamt. I don't know. Cairo—Spain. I don't remember. All night long—somewhere else. *(Beat.)* It's hot.

DIANA: Yes. Indian summer.

(MARIAN walks to the jutting edge.)

MARIAN: Dog?

DIANA: No. No dog.

(JACKMAN enters the sunroom, sees they are in garden and goes about his business.)

MARIAN: *(Litany.)* Nagasaki—Mexico City—Athens—Cairo …

DIANA: Quite a journey, mother. You did it well.

MARIAN: Did we?

DIANA: Yes. I was very proud of you.

MARIAN: I keep thinking—there's something I must do. *(Pause.)* In Cairo … there was … *(Stops.)*

DIANA: Mother? In Cairo? What.

MARIAN: A young man. I … Something.

(Music: Guitar. Step chords follow her through the following like a shadow.)

Your father. In Cairo. The staff was made up entirely of men and boys ... cooks, gardeners, drivers. The boys were messengers, mostly. Seventeen, eighteen-years old, who lived all their lives in the streets. Desperate, all of them, for money. We used them as runners. Messages. Errands. There was ... It was a time of crisis. A diplomatic crisis. Almost a war. There had been an assassination. The Americans had landed troops. The tension was palpable. Your father ... *(Beat.)* There was a secretary. I can't remember his name. One of those blond men with eyes like blue ice. Efficient enough—but dangerous. He always wore a white linen suit—but there was something secretive about him—hidden. Then I found out what it was.

(MARIAN, using the present, conjures the past. The garden becomes a courtyard in Cairo.)

In the courtyard, there was a shed. This happened in the afternoon ... The sun was blazing. I'd gone to the courtyard, thinking—I don't know—that I'd sit in the shade and read. But there was no shade. Then I remembered an umbrella—a sort of beach umbrella—the kind you stick in the sand. And I thought—well, it's in the shed ...

(MARIAN re-enacts the way she went into the shed—opening the "door" with her arm. She removes her sunglasses.)

The sun had blinded me. I couldn't see. I heard a noise—but I couldn't see what it was. And then I could.

(DIANA watches.)

One of the messenger boys—a runner—was standing in the shadows. His back was to the wall. His eyes—I can still see his eyes. He was in some kind of ecstasy. And ... the blond young man—the secretary— was kneeling in front of him ... down on his knees in his white linen suit. I didn't understand, at first. And then I did. *(Puts the sunglasses back on.)* I turned and left them without a word. I don't really know if the secretary knew I was there. But the runner—he knew. His eyes had shown me that. And it was then—because I had seen his eyes— that I knew how I could save your father. Rescue him from the danger he was in. I could bring the runner to him. Offer him to your father. After all his years of silence and suffering, "Here," I could say, "is the answer to your pain, Harry."

DIANA: And you *did* this?

MARIAN: You don't understand, Diana. I was living with a man who was dying—of denial. Do you know what that does? It kills. And I had to save his life. *I* could not save it—not as me alone. Not any more. Not in that moment. Your father loves me, Diana. But I alone was *not* the answer to his pain. *(Beat.)* In Yalta, some years later, I also led him to Mischa Andreevitch Bugarin …

DIANA: *(Pause.)* Why?

MARIAN: Why?

DIANA: Why did you bring him … men?

MARIAN: Love, Diana, does what it must. *(Beat.)* I would kill for him. If I had to.

Scene Twelve

(The garden and upper level. Morning. Sunlight. MARIAN and DIANA in place.

MAHAVOLITCH enters, having run.)

DIANA: Good morning.

MAHAVOLITCH: Yeah. Great.

DIANA: I'm going to get some coffee, mother. Do you want some?

MARIAN: Coffee? No.

(DIANA exits, passing through the sunroom. JACKMAN steps forward, but she carries on without comment.

MAHAVOLITCH moves into the garden area—where he begins to do some rudimentary end-of-run exercises, ignoring MARIAN, who seems to be lost in her own thoughts.)

MARIAN: *(Pause.)* Is it your policy, Corporal, not to speak to strangers?

MAHAVOLITCH: *(Exercising.)* No, ma'am.

MARIAN: To women wearing … *(Looks at dress.)* beige, perhaps?

MAHAVOLITCH: No, ma'am.

MARIAN: *(Removes glasses.)* Women whose eyes you cannot see?

MAHAVOLITCH: No, ma'am.

MARIAN: Why is it, then?

MAHAVOLITCH: Why is what, ma'am?

MARIAN: That you won't speak to me. Do I frighten you?

MAHAVOLITCH: *(Stops exercise.)* No, ma'am.

MARIAN: *(Pause.)* Are you a married boy?

MAHAVOLITCH: No, ma'am. And I'm not a boy, Mrs. Raymond. Anything but. I'm thirty years old.

MARIAN: Heavens! An ancient. Thirty! *(Beat.)* And not married.

MAHAVOLITCH: No, ma'am.

(MARIAN takes out a cigarette package.)

MARIAN: Not inclined? Or just not ready ...?

MAHAVOLITCH: I think that's ... I don't think that's any of your business, Mrs. Raymond.

MARIAN: *(Has selected a cigarette.)* You don't.

MAHAVOLITCH: No, ma'am.

MARIAN: Have you a light, Corporal?

MAHAVOLITCH: I don't smoke.

MARIAN: Of course not. I wasn't thinking. *(Lights cigarette.)* I dare say there's quite a lot you don't do ...

MAHAVOLITCH: *(Touch of anger.)* Ma'am?

MARIAN: You have wonderful legs.

(MAHAVOLITCH is thrown by this.)

Beautiful. In fact—you're a rather splendid specimen. *(Pointedly.)* Aren't you.

(MAHAVOLITCH is rooted, alarmed.)

What? Have I found you out?

MAHAVOLITCH: I don't understand you, Mrs. Raymond.

MARIAN: Yes, you do. Leave my husband alone.

MAHAVOLITCH: What? *(Almost laughs.)* You must be ...

MARIAN: *Leave him alone!*

(MAHAVOLITCH stares at her, then turns and begins to exit. Simultaneously, DIANA enters sunroom. MARIAN speaks to MAHAVOLITCH.)

Don't you dare do that.

(MAHAVOLITCH stops—his back to MARIAN. DIANA enters garden.)

I haven't lived ... I haven't worked all this time ... *(Begins to falter badly.)* We've worked so hard. It's been so ... difficult ...

DIANA: Mother?

(MAHAVOLITCH moves away. DIANA looks at him.)

MAHAVOLITCH: I was just leaving.

>   *(MAHAVOLITCH exits, with a final look at MARIAN.)*

DIANA: Are you all right?

MARIAN: *(Not all right.)* Yes.

DIANA: What happened?

MARIAN: Nothing happened. I lost ... I've lost ...

DIANA: Can I help? What have you lost?

MARIAN: Something. I don't know. I've lost something ...

Scene Thirteen

>   *(On the upper level, MAHAVOLITCH enters the room where HARRY sits at Marian's table.)*

MAHAVOLITCH: Sir?

HARRY: *(Not looking at him.)* Time, gentlemen. Is that it?

MAHAVOLITCH: Yessir. *(Beat.)* Is there something I could do for you, Ambassador?

HARRY: Yes. You and your friend could leave this house.

MAHAVOLITCH: You know we can't do that, sir.

>   *(MAHAVOLITCH starts to exit.)*

HARRY: Young man ...?

MAHAVOLITCH: Sir?

>   *(In the garden, MARIAN discovers her umbrella is missing.*
>   *HARRY stares at MAHAVOLITCH.)*

HARRY: ... I'll be with you presently.

MAHAVOLITCH: Sir.

>   *(MAHAVOLITCH exits.*
>   *DIANA looks for umbrella.)*

HARRY: So ...

>   *(He pours himself a drink.)*

One: Never drink in a crisis. *(Drinks.)* Two: Never admit there is a crisis. *(Drinks.)*

>   *(Hold.*
>   *Music: Flute song.)*

Scene Fourteen

(The garden and the sunroom.

DIANA enters the sunroom. The moment she is inside, JACKMAN withdraws the envelopes of photographs from her view and holds them.)

JACKMAN: I think you'll find it just there. *(The umbrella.)*

DIANA: *(Finding it.)* Thank you.

JACKMAN: She's a great one for making up the rain—isn't she—your mother.

DIANA: This time, it's the sun—and if you look, Superintendent, you'll see that it's really there.

(Starts exit.)

JACKMAN: Mrs. Marsden?

(DIANA stops.)

I'm sorry.

DIANA: No, you're not, Superintendent. But thank you for saying so.

(DIANA exits.)

JACKMAN: Damn.

(HARRY enters the sunroom.

JACKMAN is unaware of him. He looks at the envelope of photographs—and sighs.)

HARRY: Something troubles you, Superintendent?

JACKMAN: Oh. Good morning, sir. Yes—these photographs ...

(DIANA hands the umbrella to MARIAN. They exit.)

HARRY: I presume you have no taste for what they depict. I apologize.

JACKMAN: I've seen worse.

HARRY: I should hope so.

JACKMAN: What did they want of you, sir—in exchange for these?

HARRY: They wanted me to tell them how to make an atomic bomb.

JACKMAN: Please, sir ...

HARRY: What else would they want, Superintendent? I don't know why—but I have a pervasive feeling of another time and place. I keep expecting Igor Gouzenko to walk through that door ... *(Pause.)*

(MAHAVOLITCH enters, still in running gear.)

MAHAVOLITCH: Sorry to be so long. I was …

HARRY: Never apologize, Corporal. Never explain.

JACKMAN: *(Pause.)* All right, Ambassador. I think the time has come for you to look at these.

(JACKMAN hands one photo envelope to HARRY.)

Take your time.

(HARRY crosses away from him. He undoes the envelope and pulls out the pictures. He shuffles through them quickly, barely looking.)

HARRY: I've already seen these, Mister Jackman. In Moscow some time ago.

JACKMAN: I think you may not have seen them all, sir. There is one more. Here.

(JACKMAN hands over the second envelope.

HARRY, fearful of what he will see, turns away to open it.

JACKMAN watches him.)

HARRY: Oh … god …

(Suddenly, HARRY sits. Clearly, he had not known how Mischa died.

The dog barks down in the ravine.)

JACKMAN: Would you like a drink, Ambassador.

HARRY: Yes.

(JACKMAN indicates MAHAVOLITCH should take it to him. When MAHAVOLITCH holds out the drink, HARRY stares at him.)

It's not right, you know. It's not right. No one should do such things.

MAHAVOLITCH: This is for you, sir.

HARRY: Thank you. *(Takes the glass and drinks.)* In answer to your question, Superintendent—they wanted me to be their advocate here in Ottawa. It was known I would soon be returning home. They showed me the photographs—the other ones—those. The shock was not what the photographs revealed. It was not as if I was unaware of what I had done—with Mischa. The shock—the shock was that he was one of them. One of theirs. Not his own person, but someone else's person all along. That was the shock.

JACKMAN: I'm afraid it's somewhat worse than that, sir.

HARRY: Oh? How could it be?

JACKMAN: Were you not aware—are you not aware now—of your wife's part in all this?

HARRY: I beg your pardon.

JACKMAN: Your wife, Ambassador. It was she who ... provided you with Mischa.

HARRY: *(Pause.)* You're crazy.

JACKMAN: I'm afraid not, sir.

HARRY: You are crazy.

JACKMAN: No, sir. She said so herself.

HARRY: When?

JACKMAN: This morning.

HARRY: To you?

JACKMAN: She said it in the garden, sir. I have it right here, on this tape.

> *(Shows a micro-recorder.)*

HARRY: You are, of course, no better than them.

JACKMAN: Yes, sir.

HARRY: *(Looking at Mischa dead.)* Are you telling me that my wife ... What are you telling me?

JACKMAN: I merely repeat what she said. Which suggests that your wife may have been acting in conjunction with the KGB to engineer their blackmail.

> *(HARRY stares at him in disbelief.)*

Nothing is impossible, sir—given the stakes.

HARRY: Nonsense! That is absurd. I had a chance encounter with Mischa in the baths at Yalta. How is it possible my wife had even met him?

JACKMAN: Well, sir, I can only suggest she knew where to look—and there he was.

HARRY: You mean he was a prostitute?

JACKMAN: More than likely. Standing on his corner—young, attractive. Waiting.

HARRY: What you are describing, Mister Jackman, is grotesque. It is *crazy.* My wife would never betray me. Not ever.

(JACKMAN watches HARRY work his way through the details.)

I insist that—whatever she may have said—whatever she may have done—I insist that you withdraw your accusation that my wife acted in conjunction with the KGB. *I insist.* It is impossible even to begin to imagine it.

JACKMAN: Yes, sir. Accusation withdrawn. With apologies. *(Beat.)* Nevertheless, for whatever reasons, it was Mrs. Raymond who chose Mischa—and who sent him to the baths.

HARRY: And he was a plant from the KGB?

JACKMAN: Yes, sir. Well—if not a plant on the payroll, then certainly "plantable" for a fee. It's in the nature of it, isn't it, sir.

HARRY: In the nature of what?

JACKMAN: Prostitution.

HARRY: How would I know? It's more in your line of work than mine.

JACKMAN: Sorry, Ambassador. I've never used a prostitute in my life.

HARRY: Like hell you haven't. There's one standing right beside you.

MAHAVOLITCH: Hey!

JACKMAN: I think that's uncalled for, sir.

HARRY: Tell him to put his clothes on. *(To MAHAVOLITCH.)* I'm not interested in young men wearing purple running shorts.

JACKMAN: *(Quietly.)* Go and get dressed.

MAHAVOLITCH: But …

JACKMAN: *Now.*

MAHAVOLITCH: Yes, sir. *(Exits.)*

HARRY: You all work the same ploy, don't you. I guess it's in the nature of it, isn't it.

JACKMAN: *(Ignores insult.)* You still have not told me—we still have not discussed your answer, sir.

HARRY: What answer?

JACKMAN: The answer you gave the Russians—when they showed you the photographs.

HARRY: I said "no."

(JACKMAN does not respond.)

Do you think if I had said "yes," they would have done this to him?

(HARRY hands the photograph of the dead Mischa to JACKMAN, who regards it sadly. HARRY crosses away.)

That's what baffles you, isn't it, Superintendent. You must have guessed I'd said "no"—otherwise why would they kill him?

(MICHAEL enters.)

MICHAEL: All right, Superintendent. That will be all.

JACKMAN: *(Registers no surprise.)* Yes, sir.

MICHAEL: I'd like a moment alone with Ambassador Raymond. Would you mind?

JACKMAN: No, sir. Not at all.

(JACKMAN exits past MICHAEL.)

Scene Fifteen

(When JACKMAN is gone, MICHAEL moves downstage.)

HARRY: Michael. *(Beat.)* How was your party?

MICHAEL: An unqualified success—according to Juliet.

HARRY: Why are you here, Mike? Aren't they moving fast enough for you?

MICHAEL: Frankly—no. I need answers. I'm being pressed.

HARRY: The PM?

MICHAEL: No.

(When he does not elaborate, HARRY shrugs.)

HARRY: I see. Pressure from without, is that it? *(Beat.)* Still no answer? My, my. So?

MICHAEL: You let me down, Harry. I had no idea you were so vulnerable.

HARRY: Are you going to moralize?

MICHAEL: No. But I have a right to register surprise. And disappointment. I trusted you. You were the best man I had. Then *this.*

HARRY: What do you think I've done? What can you possibly think I have done?

MICHAEL: I was not aware of what you are, Harry. I was not aware of your homosexuality.

HARRY: Good.

MICHAEL: Not good. How can I say I've known you for years if I did not know that?

HARRY: Everyone has secrets. You have secrets.

MICHAEL: None that would jeopardize my country.

HARRY: *(Pause.)* I see. So—what is to be done?

MICHAEL: There are options. We must weigh them.

> *(HARRY sits on bench.)*

You could be returned to Moscow—stand trial for the murder of this boy. That is option number one.

HARRY: *(Tired.)* I did not kill him.

MICHAEL: How would you prove it?

HARRY: I could prove it with your help. If you threw the weight of the whole department behind me—if you insisted on an open trial—if the PM spoke out ...

MICHAEL: No.

HARRY: No? You know I didn't kill him! Help me. That's your job!

MICHAEL: *(Dreadful, reasoned calm.)* My job is to protect our integrity abroad. Such a trial would be a scandal, Harry. One we cannot afford. We are in a state of transition here. The PM's health—the transference of power ...

HARRY: What is the other option?

MICHAEL: You stay here—and confess.

HARRY: I did not kill him.

MICHAEL: No. You confess to having submitted to blackmail—and to having ... *(Carefully.)* foregone your oath of office.

HARRY: No! You are asking me to confess to something I did not do. Why can't you simply retire me. Recall me on compassionate grounds—because of Marian.

MICHAEL: What—and pretend that nothing happened? That I did not see those photographs? That the boy is not dead? The Soviets won't accept that, Harry. They will not accept that. And neither will I. It is a diplomatic impossibility.

HARRY: You want me to confess to something that I did not do. I did not betray my oath of office.

MICHAEL: *(Ignoring him.)* If you confess, you could then be retired ...

HARRY: No. I cannot do that.

MICHAEL: That way, we get what we want, Harry. *Silence.*

HARRY: Silence. And the boy will have died for nothing.

MICHAEL: He died for nothing, anyway. He was a throw-away. Expendable. Disposable. But the boy's death is not the problem! You are the problem! You hid this from me, Harry. You hid your weakness—your susceptibility. God knows what else is hidden in there, waiting to bring you down.

HARRY: *(Pause.)* And you with me. Yes? *(Pause.)* You're cutting me loose, aren't you. You're cutting me loose and walking away—because you can't afford to know me. You can't afford the fact that I was your friend. That you put your trust in me—that you sent me to Moscow. It doesn't matter—does it—that I did not betray your trust. That I was loyal to my posting and to my country. That couldn't matter less. All that matters is that you are standing there, poised on the brink of becoming Prime Minister—and I am here, hanging around your neck.

MICHAEL: The country, Harry. The country.

HARRY: Like hell, the country. This is all about you.

MICHAEL: *(Ignoring this.)* You have a choice to make. A murder trial—or the confession of a misdemeanour—and retirement, abroad. Surely the choice is obvious. I know what I would do. And I'm trusting you'll do the same.

HARRY: *(Quietly.)* You may know what you would do—but you don't have to do it. *I* have to do it. And I won't. To be loyal, I must appear to be disloyal—to the end of my days. Throw over everything I've stood for, all my life. No. No, Mike. No. I'd rather die. *(Pause.)* Mike. Say something. Please.

MICHAEL: *(Long pause.)* I think nothing more need be said.

(JACKMAN enters the sunroom.)

Shall I hear from you—before the day is out?

HARRY: Yes. *(Beat.)* Yes.

MICHAEL: Good-bye, then.

HARRY: Yes. Indeed. Good-bye.

(MICHAEL makes for the sunroom, where he confers with JACKMAN.)

Scene Sixteen

(DIANA and MARIAN enter. DIANA carries red maple leaves.)

DIANA: Oh—I had no idea. It's so beautiful down there. The leaves! I haven't picked leaves like this since I was a child.

MARIAN: Look, Harry. I found stones. *(Holds out hand.)* Three round, perfect stones.

(MAHAVOLITCH enters the sunroom, dressed as in Act One, with shirt and tie.

MICHAEL turns his back on MAHAVOLITCH and finishes his talk with JACKMAN.)

DIANA: Someone's visiting.

HARRY: Yes.

(MICHAEL is preparing to exit—final handshakes with JACKMAN and MAHAVOLITCH.)

DIANA: Looks like Michael.

HARRY: It is.

(MARIAN moves away—avoiding the sunroom.

MICHAEL exits along the walkway—not looking back.)

DIANA: Don't people say good-bye any more?

HARRY: Not always.

DIANA: I'm going to put these in a vase.

(DIANA exits through the sunroom.

MARIAN looks at her find.)

MARIAN: Three round, perfect stones, Harry. One for each of us. Oh ...

(HARRY watches her sadly. He crosses and takes the umbrella, which he closes.

Music: Japanese flute song.

Lights brighten—almost pure white.

MARIAN shades her eyes.)

HARRY: What is it?

MARIAN: Make the spinning *stop,* Harry. Make it stop.

HARRY: It's all right. It's all right.

MARIAN: I want—I just want to be still.

(HARRY leads her to the bench, where she sits.
Lights alter.)

Scene Seventeen

(Sunroom. JACKMAN and MAHAVOLITCH are returning files to folders.

DIANA enters with leaves in a vase. She carries them to where the flowers already sit.)

DIANA: There. Yes?

JACKMAN: Beautiful.

DIANA: Yes.

(DIANA begins to remove dead flowers from the vase.

MAHAVOLITCH goes upstage to work with papers—turning his back.)

When we met, you said you knew all about me. Everything. Down there—walking with my mother, I was thinking about your having said that. And what I knew about myself before all this began. And what I know now. And what I don't know. And it occurred to me that, one day, it might be interesting if you were to examine others in the light of what you know about yourself. That's what I intend to do. At least—I'm going to try. I just thought I'd say so.

(Takes dead flowers and exits.

Sunroom lights begin to fade.)

JACKMAN: Interesting woman.

MAHAVOLITCH: *(Smiling.)* Yeah.

JACKMAN: Dangerous.

(Lights fade completely.)

Scene Eighteen

(Garden. MARIAN seated on the bench—DIANA on the sunroom steps—HARRY slowly pacing to one side.

JACKMAN and MAHAVOLITCH in the sunroom, filing papers.)

MARIAN: Where are we now, Harry? A garden somewhere. I love it here. In any garden anywhere, I feel as if I can breathe again … and the sun. Here we are—at the top of a hill. There's a river down there.

We've been here before, I know we have—but I don't know when. Not that it matters. *When* doesn't matter any more. *Where* doesn't matter. *(Beat.)* I want … something. Something is missing. What can it be? Are you there?

HARRY: Yes.

MARIAN: How old are we, Harry, now?

HARRY: I don't remember.

MARIAN: Nagasaki … Athens … Cairo …

HARRY: *(Finishing litany.)* Moscow. Yes.

    (HARRY crosses down and puts his hand on her shoulder.)

MARIAN: Is that you?

HARRY: Yes. Is that you?

MARIAN: Yes.

    (HARRY kisses the top of her head.

    The dog barks in the ravine.)

We're alive, Harry.

HARRY: Yes. We're alive.

    (MARIAN arranges her stones on the bench in the sun.

    MAHAVOLITCH exits.)

MARIAN: Do you forgive me?

HARRY: Why? What for?

MARIAN: Something I did. I don't know … Mischa. Is that right?

HARRY: Not to worry. It's over, now. Done with. *(Beat.)* I love you, Marian.

    (DIANA looks at her parents.)

What a long time it's been. What a long life we've had—together and apart. Alone and together. Before there was you—before that, I … *(Stops—begins again.)* All my life, I've been a diplomat. Born in a pinstripe suit. First word I said was "no." Carefully. Carefully. Stood with my arms at my sides. Always at *attention*. Look at me right now, Diana. Yes? Must have been the very first view you had of your father: *man at attention*. Pinstripes. Waiting … Standing at attention, waiting for someone else—always someone else—to make the first move. Even you, Diana. "Are you my father?" *(Smiles.)* Yes. I am.Yes—I am.

MARIAN: *(Not moving.)* I love you, Harry.

HARRY: Yes. You love me. *(Beat.)* Yes. You love me. *(Beat.)* What a piece of news that was, the first time I heard it! *Marian loves me ...* *(Beat.)* Not like the first news I had. The very first news I received was that my parents had died. I was six years old. Six. "There's been an accident," someone said. "There's been ... a terrible accident." *(Beat.)* And my guardian—my uncle said to me: "I will show you how to survive." Stand up straight—stare life in the face—and tell it you have come to bargain for terms. When it says "I want you—just as you are"—tell it "No—not without terms." Negotiate. Diplomacy. Restraint. But I was ... I was I. Me: hidden. What you have to learn, I discovered, is how to hide out in the open. That was the bargain. Those were the terms. *Don't.* Then I fell in love—a long, long ago—with Francis Oliver. That was when I made my choice. To live incognito. And so, we never embraced. We never touched. I never held him—never. Francis knew, of course—knew that I loved him. I'll never know if he loved me. But he said to me: "You are my stillborn lover, Harry." True. Yes. True. And he went to Spain and died. Leaving me with everything unsaid. Until I met you.

MARIAN: I love you, Harry.

HARRY: Yes. And I—dear God, how I love you. But I have been your stillborn lover, too, passing through your life on a diplomatic passport ...

MARIAN: What is it, Harry? What's the matter? Why are you crying?

HARRY: I'm not. I never cry. *(Pause.)* I hope you heard what I said. I hope you can hear me.

MARIAN: Yes. I can hear you.

HARRY: I want to tell you something, Marian.

MARIAN: Yes.

HARRY: Diana, would you be good enough to get your Mother and me a drink?

DIANA: Of course.

    (DIANA goes to sunroom drinks table.)

HARRY: For our life together—for our lives—I thank you.

MARIAN: Yes. *(Pause.)* The dog has stopped barking, Harry.

HARRY: Yes. It has.

MARIAN: *(Pause.)* Harry?

HARRY: Yes?

MARIAN: Are we saying good-bye?

HARRY: *(Pause.)* Yes.

MARIAN: I'm afraid. Are you?

HARRY: A little.

MARIAN: May we sit—for just a moment?

HARRY: Of course.

> *(He sits beside her. MARIAN hands him one of the stones.)*

MARIAN: Here. It's your move.

> *(The lights alter to isolate them.)*

Coda

(DIANA and JACKMAN remain in place.

MICHAEL, JULIET and MAHAVOLITCH enter onto the walkways.)

MARIAN: *(Voice over.)* When the game of Go is over, the one who loses must approach the Master of Go and ask him: "Where did I go wrong?" The Master always replies with the same answer: "Where did you go wrong? Everywhere."

(They all freeze.

Music: Three final chords.

Lights dim.

The play ends.)

Nov. 8

11, 28, 29 34 38 40 48

2 5 18 24 40 45 9

3, 19, 26, 39